THROUGH THE WORMHOLE

THROUGH THE
WORMHOLE

ROBERT J. FAVOLE

FLYWHEEL
PUBLISHING

Publisher's Cataloging-in-Publication
(Provided by Quality Books, Inc.)

Favole, Robert J.
    Through the wormhole / by Robert J. Favole — 1st ed.
    p. cm.
    Audience: Age 10 and older
    SUMMARY: Being African American, Michael encounters racial stereotyping by classmates who find it unusual for non-whites to participate in equestrian sports. Kate—who is not African American—is a swimmer. One day the two friends are contacted by a riding instructor—who is supposed to be dead! He leaves them computer software which enables the pair to travel back in time to the Revolutionary War where Michael meets his ancestor, an American cavalryman. Michael and Kate must not only make sure that Michael's ancestor survives the war, they must also warn newly arrived General Lafayette of a kidnapping plot.
    LCCN 00-106131
    ISBN 1-930826-00-1

    1. United States—History—Revolution, 1775–1783—Juvenile fiction.   2. United States—History—Revolution, 1775–1783—Participation, Afro-American—Juvenile fiction.   3. Time travel—Juvenile fiction.   4. Self-acceptance—Juvenile fiction. I. Title.

PZ7.F2795Thr2001   [Fic]
                                            QBI00–901370

For Cynthia,

who makes all things possible

and infinitely better.

Acknowledgments

Deepest thanks to my family for unflagging support and faith. Special thanks to our son, Kristian, for his uplifting loyalty, love for the written word, and considerable editorial skills.

Thanks to lifelong friend, John Cardone, for his willingness to help.

My appreciation goes to Jon Errek for reading the manuscript to his class at Alta Vista School. And thanks to the class members for their attention, enthusiasm and comments.

Thanks to those who read various drafts and provided comment and encouragement, in particular, Jean Fritz, whose admirable openness sets a fine standard.

Finally, thanks to editors Stephanie Jacob Gordon and Judith Ross Enderle of Writers Ink for their untangling and encouragement.

one

Kate, get out of there. The rest of you, give me ten."

Kate climbed out of the pool. The other swimmers pushed off, two to a lane. Kate grabbed a towel and followed Coach Sanders to the bleachers.

"Sit down, I want to talk to you." He sat with elbows on knees watching his team swim the warmup laps. "I've been thinking about what happened the other day. You know what I'm talkin' about?"

Kate looked down. She had been afraid of this. "I guess so." She ran a finger over the tightly parallel ridges in the metal bleachers.

"I know you weren't sick. What really happened?"

"Not sure." Kate's voice was thin.

"Was it nerves? You are a freshman. Your first high school meet and all."

"I don't know."

"Well, you'd better start figuring it out. And you'd better decide whether or not you want to be on this team. If you do, it's a commitment to your teammates, to me and to yourself."

Tears welled in Kate's eyes. She swallowed hard and pursed her lips. "Am I off the team?"

"That depends on you. You take today off from practice and think about it. Because we can't have any more episodes like that. You understand?"

"Yes." But really she wasn't sure.

Coach Sanders stood and walked to poolside, watching his swimmers and barking corrections.

Kate sat alone. She shivered. Was this his way to cut her from the team?

She made the long walk to the locker room and changed out of her bathing suit. The locker room was empty and quiet. So different from a few minutes before when it had pulsated with the chatter and energy of the team. The smell of chlorine became suddenly stifling. She hurried. She might still catch up with Michael.

The hallway was teeming. Kids bustled this way or that. Others sauntered, in no rush to leave now that they were finally free to go. Kate weaved her way through the crowd. Michael was rummaging in his locker.

"Hi."

Michael looked up. "Hey, Kate. No practice?"

"Not today."

Michael stuck his face back in the locker. "Can't find that math sheet. It's got to be in here. I've looked everywhere."

Every so often a wadded sheet of paper jumped out of his locker.

Kate leaned against the wall and took in all the action. Through the crowd, she glimpsed her friend Shauna. She raised her hand to wave, but too late. Shauna headed out the door. Kate's hand was stranded for a moment in midair. She pretended she had meant to smooth her hair. Her hand shied back to her side and her face flushed. She lowered her chin to hide her blushing behind the reddish-gold fall of her hair.

When she peeked out from behind her hair, Michael was still searching. The crowd was still getting on. So, no one had noticed. She breathed again. Her face cooled. She straightened up and tucked her hair behind her ears, on purpose this time.

The crowd seemed to part as Jamal and James swaggered up the hallway, pants all baggy. They did everything as though they were taking center stage, in the spotlight. Always together. "Jamal-n-James", as though it were one word. And everyone knew them.

Jamal was average height. He had broad shoulders. His walk was like a dance. Everything about Jamal shined. His brown eyes were piercing. His dark skin glistened.

James was tall and lanky, with buzzed blonde hair. His shoes scuffed along the floor with every step. Everything about James was dull. His hair didn't shine. His blue eyes had no luster. His skin was flat pale.

They were heading right toward Kate. They'd never even noticed her before. But here the spotlight came right for her. What would she say? What would they say? Not freshmen hazing, please.

But they walked right past Kate. Right to Michael. As though she wasn't even there.

"Hey, it's the wannabe white boy?"

Michael turned from the locker. "Hey, Jamal."

"What you got in there? Your little red riding suit?" Jamal grinned.

A few kids paused to check out the action.

"Yeah, right. And the big, bad wolf, too." Michael tried to smile, but his eyes were hard.

"Why do you call him white?" James asked.

"You know, because even though he's black on the outside, he's white on the inside." Jamal turned toward Michael. "That true?" Jamal poked Michael in the chest.

More kids stopped. A small crowd encircled them, huddling in. Kate couldn't breathe.

Michael knocked Jamal's finger away with his forearm.

"Light him up, Jamal," someone said from the crowd.

Kate felt as though if she fainted she wouldn't even fall, propped up by the press of the crowd.

Jamal's cousin André pushed through the crowd. "What's up, Jamal?"

"Bro man here wants to be a country club white boy. He dresses like a *de*luxe stable *boy* and they let him race. And if he wins, they let him come in and be the house *boy*."

Michael was beginning to sweat. His mouth drooped, but his eyes were still cold. "Yeah, right," he said.

"Leave him alone, dawg," André said.

Jamal shrugged. "I'm just playin' wit' you, Michael." He turned and the crowd parted. He dance-walked away.

"Later, wannabe." James shuffled after him.

As the crowd drifted away, its voices murmured. "Prep." "Dumb freshman." The comments were darts.

"Don't mind that stuff, Michael." André walked away.

Michael seemed in shock. He just stood there.

"Let's go, Michael." Kate grabbed wads of paper from the floor.

Michael slammed the locker door.

"How's he even know you ride?" Kate asked.

"He saw me on the way to a meet. Red jacket, white pants, the whole thing. Now he's calling me white 'cause I don't do like him."

"Those guys think they're so cool and all that," Kate said. Unfortunately so did everyone else.

She followed Michael onto the bus, all the way to the back where no one else was sitting. Kate slid into the seat next to him. She stared at the brushed silver letters of Brookville High School, but she was picturing Michael in his riding clothes, sitting tall on his horse, poised to start. She would cheer as Michael raced, clearing every hurdle.

The bus rumbled away from the curb, shaking Kate from her daydream.

"I can't believe all I said was 'Yeah, right.' I sounded like a fool."

"No you didn't. What else could you do?"

"I could quit?"

"School?"

"No. Riding."

"Just because of Jamal?"

"It isn't just Jamal. It's other people, too. When I go to a meet, everybody else is white. Most people are nice, but some look at me weird. Like, what are you doing here? Then I hear stuff from the crowd. Just like today." Michael looked out the window.

"You never said anything."

"It's a hard thing to talk about."

Kate knew exactly what he meant.

"And sometimes I don't feel right at the meets," Michael spoke toward the window. "Like Jamal says, a wannabe. Maybe I should quit. Play basketball instead. Then Jamal won't hassle me."

"But you love to ride."

"Yeah. Especially competing. But it'd be easier just to quit. Stop having to deal with everybody's attitudes, laying down all these expectations. If I ride, I'm trying to act white."

"That's just dumb."

"Maybe, but that's the way it is." Michael looked out the window.

"What you said about things being hard to talk about . . ."

He turned toward her. "Yeah."

"I never told you how bad things have gotten on swim team. I feel like quitting, too."

"Why, you're getting so fast."

"Only during practice. But it's not about that."

"What then?"

Kate looked down at her wringing hands. "I get so nervous before a race, I feel like I'm going to throw up." She glanced up and caught his eye for a moment. "It gets worse on the starting blocks. I freeze up. Can't breathe. I get dizzy and everything closes in. I feel like—-paralyzed. If I dive, I'll drown. It happened the other day."

"You were afraid of the water?"

"No, I love the water. But it's like a giant fist is squeezing me and I feel I won't be able to move."

"You dive anyway?"

"No. I told them I was sick and they scratched me from the races. I can't do this anymore."

"What's it about?"

"I don't know. The pressure, I guess. Do you get nervous before a meet?"

"Yeah, but once I start the ride it turns to thrill. Rudy taught me to just go for it. He'd say, 'It's an adventure. Make of it what you will.'"

"What does that mean?"

"That it's up to you how serious or fun you make it."

Would she ever be able to do that with swimming? Or anything? "You miss Rudy a lot, huh?"

"Yeah, the Star's not the same."

"At least he was doing what he loved."

"Definitely. He lived exactly how he wanted, tending horses. He was ninety-three when he . . . "

"Are you going to the Star today?" she asked.

"Yeah. Wanna come?"

"If I can."

The bus rattled around the last turn before their stop. Kate stood, anxious to get going. As she adjusted the straps of her backpack, the bus driver heavy-footed the brakes. The momentum threw her forward. She bounded down the aisle, swung around the pole and jumped down the steps. Michael was right behind her.

Kate ran up the front steps and flung open the door.

"Hi, Mom."

"Hi, Kitten," her mother called from upstairs.

"Can I go to the Lucky Star with Michael?"

"Okay. Say hi for me."

"I will." Kate slammed the door behind her and ran to the garage to get her bike. She rolled around to the front of Michael's house. The door opened.

"Good afternoon, young lady." Michael's father had a deep voice. The care he took with every syllable made his greeting seem like an embrace.

"Hi, Mr. B."

"Great day for a ride, Kitten." Mr. B smiled.

Kate nodded. Only Mr. B and her parents called her that. It was nice. So was Mr. B's smile. It was just a little bit crooked, curling a touch higher on one side. And his twinkling eyes gave him a funny, mischievous look.

Michael pedaled his bike around to the front.

"Hi, Michael," Mr. B said.

"Hey," Michael droned.

"Something wrong, Michael?"

"No." Michael didn't sound convincing.

Mr. B considered him for a moment. "Well, you kids have fun."

"Thanks, Mr. B."

They rode at a lazy pace onto Old Lark Lane, a winding country road that led to the Lucky Star Stables. A row of oak trees lined Old Lark, and behind the oaks horses grazed against a backdrop of rolling hills.

They turned onto the Star's long, gravel driveway, rolling under a canopy of trees to a pasture gate. Jonathan Apples was waiting.

"Hey Johnny," Michael called. His voice had its lilt back.

The big brown horse flung his head up and down.

"He's trying to tell you something," Kate said.

"Yeah, like 'it's about time.'"

As they propped their bikes against the fence, Johnny leaned over and took a bit of Michael's hair between his lips.

Michael pulled away.

Johnny snorted.

"And now he's laughing." Michael shook his head. "I'm telling you, this horse has a sense of humor."

They walked Johnny down the path to the barn where Pauline, owner of the Lucky Star, was loading tack into her Jeep.

"Hi, you two. How's Johnny? Told any good jokes lately?"

"You just missed his stand up act." Michael smiled crookedly, just like his father.

"You wanna come up to the arena and see our new thoroughbred?" Pauline asked.

"Maybe later. We're going for a ride. Can we saddle Midnight for Kate?"

"Sure." Pauline hopped into the Jeep.

"Thanks," Michael said. "We'll be on the upper trail."

"Okay. You'll be here for your lesson tomorrow?"

"I'll be here, Coach," Michael said.

"Great. 'Til tomorrow then." She drove off toward the arena.

The upper trail started just beyond the barn and became steep almost immediately. The rocky path was edged with scrubby bushes. Michael and Johnny led the way.

After a couple of minutes, the trail opened onto a broad meadow.

"Johnny wants to run," Michael said.

"I'm gonna take it slow. You go on."

"Okay. Meet you at the creek."

Johnny sprang into a gallop. They seemed almost in flight, except for Johnny's pounding hooves and the divots they threw.

Kate held Midnight to a walk. The sun's warmth felt good. The grass was green and soft. A hawk, with her striped tail fanned, glided silently above. With a few wing beats, the bird soared.

Kate exhaled deeply. The tension of the day drifted away. No wonder Michael loved riding so much. And the Star.

Before Kate reached the creek, Michael and Johnny were jumping a series of rough hewn hurdles on the meadow's edge. Michael leaned close to Johnny's neck as the horse rose, pulling up his forelegs and hind legs in turn and flowing over the stacked logs. It was awesome. After the final hurdle, they turned and galloped back to Kate.

"Johnny's really kickin' it today." Michael's eyes twinkled. Just like Mr. B's.

After their ride, they said goodbye to Johnny and fetched their bikes from the fence. They pedaled down the Star's long driveway and turned onto Old Lark Lane, side by side.

A tall hedgerow loomed on the right where a dirt road joined Old Lark. From behind the hedge, an engine rumbled. Kate and Michael jumped off their bikes and yielded toward the left shoulder.

The engine roared. An old pickup truck lurched onto Old Lark, skidded, then lumbered away, leaving them in a squall of clatter and dust.

Michael dropped to his knees. His bike fell. His face went blank, jaw dropping.

"Michael, are you okay?"

He swallowed hard, then mumbled. "Did you see that?"

"What?" Obviously, she had seen the truck.

"That was—Rudy's truck, and . . . "

"Michael?"

"I saw the driver in the big side mirror. It was—Rudy."

Michael sat dazed on the grass along the roadside. He felt like he'd been punched in the stomach. A storm of confusion whirled in his head. Tension from school mingled with exhilaration from riding Johnny. Now this. But a question gnawed at him through the confusion. Why that truck on that road at that moment? The driver must have waited for them. He had wanted Michael to see him. But why that dirt road? Because the truck had come from Rudy's old house. What kind of a prank was this? He was going to find out.

"That dirt road goes to Rudy's old house. His grandson lives there now," Michael said.

"Well, he probably has Rudy's truck and that was him driving. He just looks like Rudy."

"I don't think so. He's got to be sixty or seventy years younger." Michael didn't buy it. The questions were pushing him. "Let's ride down there and see if he's home."

"Why? You don't really think that was Rudy. I mean, he's dead." Kate sounded a little spooked.

"I know. Couldn't be. But I wanna see if his grandson still has the truck. It's okay if you don't want to go. I'll meet you at home."

"No. It's all right. I'm coming."

They pedaled down the dirt road for a mile or so, passing an occasional house, until they came to a cottage on the right.

Michael hopped off of his bike. "This is it. I was here a lot with Rudy."

The cottage was small, maybe two or three rooms. It was bordered by a low, old fashioned iron fence. Behind it loomed a barn, large by contrast to the house. A man was sitting at a table in the single large window facing the road. When he noticed them, he came to the door.

"Hey, you're Michael, right? My grandfather talked about you all the time. He took me to see you ride."

The guy looked like he was twenty-five or thirty. He was built like Rudy, small and wiry, but any family resemblance ended in his smooth face. Rudy's had been all deep wrinkles and crags. Maybe he'd look like Rudy in sixty years.

"So, Rudy was your grandfather?" Michael said.

"Yeah, I'm Mark. Old Granddad was a gem. I sure miss him."

"Me, too," Michael said. "This is my friend, Kate."

"Nice to meet you," Mark said.

"You, too," Kate said.

"Hey, Mark, do you know what happened to Rudy's old truck?" Michael felt electricity in the air.

"I sure do." Mark stepped out of the little gate. "I've got it right back there in the barn. Want to see?"

"Yeah, please," Michael said.

"Come on." Mark walked toward the barn. "I don't use it much, but I start it up every now and then just to keep it running." He reached for the handle of the barn door.

Michael's nerves crackled.

Mark swung the door open. "What the . . . ?"

No truck. The barn was packed and stacked with all manner of old stuff. But in a space just right for the truck, there was no truck.

"I usually keep the key in it. Guess I shouldn't have. But who would come back here and steal an old thing like that? Damn! Hey, why'd you want to know about it, anyway?"

"Because I think we just saw it about ten minutes ago pulling onto Old Lark," Michael said.

"Did you see who was in it?"

Michael glanced at Kate. Couldn't say something wild like your dead grandfather was driving it. "Looked like an old guy."

"Well, I don't know who that could be. Damn! Guess I'll have to call the police." Mark kicked the dirt. "Damn!"

"I hope you get it back," Michael said.

"Yeah. Thanks. And thanks for stopping by to let me know."

"No problem."

"Take it easy," Mark said.

"You too."

Michael and Kate pedaled back toward Old Lark.

"Michael, you don't think you saw a ghost or something?"

"No. But I don't know exactly what to think. It's just too weird." The truck had been coming from Mark's house—Rudy's house. But who was driving? Michael couldn't admit to himself just how sure he was that it had been Rudy.

"Probably one of Rudy's old friends borrowed the truck and he just looked like Rudy," Kate said.

"Probably," Michael said. But why hadn't Mark known about it? "We'll probably never know." But Michael was dying to know. On the other hand, he would probably learn more only if there were more scamming. And what kind of scam could it be? Aimed at him? His family? Pauline?

When they turned the corner onto their street, things turned even weirder. The old pickup was parked in front of Michael's house.

Michael's scalp tingled. He streaked down the street and skidded to a stop next to the driver's door. No one was inside. He was in a panic. What about his parents? And his little brother Jacob? He dropped his bike and ran up the steps. Kate was right behind him. "Mom?" No answer. "Dad?" The back door slammed.

They ran down the hall into the kitchen. Empty.

Michael flung open the back door and ran into the yard. All quiet except for the wind chimes playing on the breeze. And nothing else was moving.

"Michael, check this out," Kate called from the kitchen.

She handed him a small, cardboard box.

"It was right here on the counter."

Michael looked at its hand-printed label. It said, "For Michael and Kate. Make of it what you will."

"Rudy," he whispered. "What's the deal here?" Who could know Rudy had said that to him a thousand times?

The ignition of an engine snapped Michael from his thoughts. He and Kate exchanged a glance before dashing back to the front door. Michael yanked it open in time to see the old pickup rattling down the street. A hand, extended from the driver's window, waved goodbye.

Michael's mind raced. Chase the truck? He'd never catch it. Call the police? And say what, I just saw a truck stolen by a ghost? Call Mark? Then he remembered the box. "I don't believe this." His hands jittered as he unfolded the wings of the boxtop and lifted the lid. It was full of computer stuff. He pulled out a disk. "Cyber—Time—Surfers," he read aloud. The initials "CTS" were styled to look like a surfer on a board marked like the face of a clock. He handed the disk to Kate.

"Ever hear of it?" she asked.

"No." Michael lifted more from the box. "And this is virtual reality gear. Two sets. Never seen anything as high-tech."

He handed Kate a small wristband with two buttons, then what looked like sci-fi sunglasses with built-in earphones.

"Let's check this out," Michael said.

Kate followed Michael back to the kitchen.

From the small desk in the corner, he took a telephone book and leafed through it. He settled on a page and ran one finger down a column. He dialed a number and pressed the speaker button. A phone rang on the other end.

"The Software Company, may I help you?"

"Yes, do you have any software called Cyber—Time—Surfers?"

"Nothing like that in stock. Let me plug into our on-line catalogues. Can you hold?"

"Sure."

In a minute the clerk's voice was back. "Can't find

any software by that name. No company listing, either. Are you sure you have the name right?"

"Yeah."

"Where did you hear about it?"

"Ah—from a friend. Thanks anyway."

"And thank you for calling The Software Company." The line went dead.

Kate strapped on the wristband. "What are these buttons for?"

"The black one probably controls the direction you move. See the little arrows? I don't know about the red one. The manual's probably in the software. Maybe it'll explain all this weird stuff going on." Michael was still in conflict, dying to find out, but dreading to know. "Let's go up to my room and run this."

Michael put the disk in his computer.

"I've never done virtual reality before. Is this going to be okay?" Kate asked.

"It's just a computer program. We'll check it out, then shut it down. Don't worry, it'll be fine."

With their headgear and wristbands on, Michael and Kate found themselves in a virtual reality hallway lined with doors as far as they could see. Using the black buttons, they moved down the hallway. Michael tried the doors on the left, Kate those on the right. Each one had a date printed in bold white: April 24, 1863, June 21, 1942, October 3, 1609. The dates seemed in no particular order. And not a single door would open.

"Michael!"

Pressing the black arrow button, he moved to where Kate stood at a door marked "May 19, 1778."

"This one opens." She turned the knob gingerly and swung the door wide.

Light flooded into the dim hallway from a sort of round tunnel. The light was distorted like heat waves reflecting off a hot road. Through the wavy distortion, they saw a mossy, stone wall rambling by an old farmhouse and barn. A gentle breeze carried the smells of spring. Impossible. No way! Through that door it wasn't virtual reality. It was—actual reality.

"Michael, that looks real."

"Couldn't be. Just great graphics," Michael said. But somehow it was real.

On the wall beside the door, a video screen began to glow pale green. "Touch here to get started," blinked in black.

"It's the manual," Michael said. At his touch, the letters disappeared and the screen showed an animated CTSurfer on his clock/surfboard cresting a wave of flipping calendar pages. As the surfer finished his ride, the picture faded. Michael's heart raced.

An image appeared on the screen. Michael stumbled backwards. It was a movie of Rudy brushing a horse at his cottage. Right where they had been that afternoon.

Kate grabbed Michael's arm. "Okay, Michael," her voice trembled, "let's shut it down."

Michael couldn't answer. He was spellbound.

Rudy looked toward them, patted the horse, and

walked to the foreground until his craggy face filled the screen.

"Greetings, CyberTimeSurfers. You're probably surprised to see me. Well, this whole thing has been surprising to me, too, I'll tell ya." Rudy laughed.

"And you're probably wondering how. Well, let me start at the beginning. A few days ago two guys came to see me. They said they wanted me to tape a little speech to you about a CyberTimeSurfing mission. I didn't know what the heck they were talking about. And I was more than a little suspicious, I'll tell ya. When they told me you two would be time traveling, well, I went to throw them off my land. But they said it was life and death and they just needed a few minutes to prove themselves to me.

"To make a long story short, they put this gear on me." Rudy held up the headgear. "And gosh durnit, I traveled back to my youth—for just a minute—but long enough to prove it to me, so I listened to these guys some more.

"They said you two need to travel into the past to— *fulfill* the present. They asked me to make this tape because you know you can trust me. They tell me you will be seeing this tape a year after I've made it. I told these guys I wanted to time travel one more time, into the future, so I could be the one to bring you this gear. So strangers wouldn't be coming into your home. And if you are watching this tape, I guess you got the gear okay.

"Now, when you walk through that door, you'll be in the countryside outside of Philadelphia. And it'll be May 19, 1778, late in the afternoon. It'll be the middle of the Revolutionary War.

"Listen up, kids. This is serious and dangerous, but it's got to be done.

"The British are planning to trap the Marquis de Lafayette. He's French. An aristocrat. One of the richest men in France. Barely more than a boy—just twenty—but he's already a full fledged general in the Continental Army. He came here to fight for America's independence. He's been risking his life and spending his fortune for about a year now. If he's captured, the alliance between France and the United States will fall apart and we'll lose the War.

"Okay, why you? I asked that, too, believe me. It turns out that saving Lafayette is only part of the mission. Michael, your great, great, great," Rudy counted on his fingers, "great, great, great grandfather, John Banks, is a cavalryman. He's with Lafayette. If John is killed, that will be the end of the Banks. Let me be plain. If John dies in 1778, his son, your great, great, great, great, great grandfather, won't be born and so on, right down to you, Michael. You get my drift? To preserve, er, fulfill, the present you've got to go." Rudy squared his face to the screen. He looked deadly serious. "That's why this is critical. You've got to save Lafayette and John. Both of you.

"The doorway there leads into a small storage room.

It's attached to the side of an abandoned farmhouse. To get home, you have to press the red button while you're in that storage closet." Rudy tipped his face and squinted one eye. "If you lose that gear or if it breaks, you can't get home. Simple as that. You can't get home! Forewarned is forearmed.

"I expect you've got questions. You can chat with the CTS guys by pressing the button on the bottom of the screen.

"Oh, yes, there's a little somethin' for you in the barn. And remember, this is your chance. Make of it what you will. And good luck."

The picture flickered and dissolved to a green glow.

A button on the bottom of the screen blinked, "Connect to CTSI."

Kate could see Michael was drawn to the button. Its dangers repelled her.

Michael reached for it, but Kate grabbed his hand.

"Wait!"

"For what? We've got to get some answers," Michael said.

Kate couldn't process all this through her fear, like a stark light in her brain. "You said you'd shut it down. Just a computer program."

"I know what I said, but that was Rudy. Nobody could fake that. And you heard what he said. We've got to go on line and see what these CTS guys can tell us. And Rudy said *both* of us."

Kate tried to catch her breath. Michael's words were an avalanche, coming so fast. She fixated on the last. "But why both of us? Rudy only mentioned your family."

"That's the first thing we'll ask them. If you're not okay with it, you can always take the gear off. You'd be safe and on your way home."

Abandoning Michael. Waiting in her room. While Michael—did what? That was impossible. She was stuck between a fear and an impossibility. "Okay, go ahead."

Michael pressed the button. The screen flashed the message, "connecting to CTSI," while a tiny, animated hourglass slowly turned.

In a minute, the screen filled with the image of a young man sitting at a table.

"Hello Michael and Kate. Glad to see you. I'm with the CyberTimeSurfing Institute. Call me Mack. Please excuse me for not properly introducing myself. Security concerns prevent me. I assume you have questions."

"Definitely," Michael said. "First, why both of us?"

"Because alone you would have no chance. Even together there is no guarantee you'll succeed, or even make it back. But alone, no chance."

"And if we don't succeed?" Michael asked.

"The Banks line will end in 1778. History would be altered and, Michael, you would cease to exist."

"Cease to exist? I don't get it. I'm here, so my ancestor must have survived. Why do we need to go back to fix what obviously turned out all right the first time?"

"Michael, there is no *first time*, There is only *the time*."

"I still don't get it."

"Everything can turn out all right, as you put it, only with your help. That's the paradox of time travel. The present, as you know it, does not happen without your intervention in the past—to fulfill the present. If you don't successfully intervene, the present can—will—be altered."

Michael shook his head. "Bottom line is, things can only turn out if I go?"

"Yes, well, if you both go."

"And you've invented a time machine?" Michael asked.

"CTSI has, yes."

"Who the heck is CTSI?" Michael asked.

"The CyberTimeSurfing Institute is a group of physicists, computer scientists and historians. We have developed a way to travel through time using wormholes, accessible through the computer.

"What are wormholes?" Kate stuttered. Sounded dark, dank and dirty.

"Think of them as tunnels through space and time.

They were predicted by Einstein's relativity equations. Having mastered the laws of quantum gravity, we at CTSI have learned how to manipulate wormholes so that one may enter the mouth of a wormhole at a certain place and time and exit the other end at a different place and time."

"You're kidding," Michael said.

"No, Michael, I'm dead serious. I know it sounds far fetched, but it's not. It's consistent with the laws of gravity. Consider that you saw Rudy today, about a year after his death."

"Why all the tricks to get us here?" Michael asked.

"We deem it necessary to keep secret the Institute and CyberTimeSurfing to avoid exploitation by those who would use time travel to advance some personal agenda, be it political, financial or otherwise. We enlisted Rudy because you trusted him. We knew he would get the equipment to you, making sure it didn't fall into the wrong hands. And he did just that."

"If you need secrecy, why tell us all about it?"

"Well, Michael, first because yours is a rare case where it is absolutely necessary. If we didn't explain, you wouldn't go through the wormhole. Or you wouldn't appreciate the gravity of the situation. Second, even if you chose to—spill the beans, so to speak—no one would believe you. We believe our secret is safe enough, or more precisely, that the necessity outweighs the risk."

"What do we have to do, exactly?" Kate asked.

"I don't know exactly. You will have to play it out as it comes. It's life, only it's life in the past. You must simply see that Lafayette escapes the trap and that Private John Banks lives to see dawn on May 21."

"Sounds real simple." Michael's voice had a sarcastic edge.

"It'll be dangerous?"

"Yes, Kate. You will be in a war zone facing all the risks that entails. Life and death. But, for Michael, his father and brother, it will be more dangerous if you choose not to go through the wormhole. And the world would be sorry to lose Michael's future contributions."

"If John Banks dies—so will I?"

"You will cease to exist. Call it death if you wish."

"How do you know that?" Michael asked.

"Our historians have discovered a very small number of events in the past that require intervention in order to come out—right, so to speak. That is, to come out in a way that supports the present. And this is one of them."

"What's it like to go through the wormhole? You have to crawl or something?" Kate asked.

"Oh no. You walk. It's comfortable. It feels no different than walking down any hallway, except, as you can see, light oscillates in the wormhole, so things look a little rippled and sometimes bluish."

"And what happens when we come back?" Michael asked.

"If you return to the present, you will exit the mouth of the wormhole and reenter the virtual hallway. We will manipulate the wormhole so that you return only a few minutes later than when you first left. Of course, you must have your gear to get back. And you must return by noon on the twenty-first. That's as long as we can hold the wormhole open. It consumes enormous amounts of energy. The digital readout in the lower right of your field of vision will tell you how much longer you have until noon on the twenty-first."

"And if we don't make it before the timer reaches zero?" Kate asked.

"Then you will live out your lives in the eighteenth century."

Mack's answer dropped a curtain of silence.

"No more questions?"

Michael and Kate exchanged a glance.

"Can we talk about it for a few minutes?" Michael asked.

"For a few minutes only. Can't hold the wormhole open."

"Okay, thanks—I guess," Michael said.

"Good luck," Mack said. The screen went blank.

"Come on, Kate, let's go back and talk."

She followed Michael down the hallway, then took off her head gear. She was standing next to Michael in front of his desk.

"We've got some fast figuring to do," Michael said.

"What do you mean?" Kate felt empty. Her nervousness would come back later, she knew. But right then she was calm.

"If it's the way Mack and Rudy say it is, then I've got to go, no question. But doesn't this seem, I don't know, like a little too much? A little over the top?"

"Yeah. But all the high-tech stuff nowadays is like that if you think about it. And like you said, that was Rudy. Nobody could fake that close-up."

"That was Rudy, no question. And I've always trusted him, back to when I was little."

"And if things are the way Mack said, and we don't go through the wormhole, you and Jacob and your dad. . . I couldn't stand that." Kate's stomach began to tighten. "We've got to go."

"I feel bad dragging you into this, Kate. It's not your problem."

"You didn't drag me, they did. And your family is like a second family to me, anyway. We've lived next door for so long."

"Yours, too."

"Michael, I wouldn't ditch you no matter what."

He looked her straight in the eyes. "Thanks, Kate."

She wanted to lighten Michael's mood, and buoy her own courage. "Shall we take a stroll into 1778?"

Michael smiled. "Okay, let's go. But no strolling. We've got to haul. Got to be back by noon on the twenty-first."

They put their headgear on and walked back down

the hallway. Their door was closed. Michael reached for the knob and pulled it open to the wrinkly vision of the farmhouse.

Michael turned to Kate. "Ready?"

Her knotted stomach started jumping. She tried to sound flip. "All righty then. Let's go."

Michael stepped through the door and into the mouth of the wormhole. Kate was right behind him.

Just as Mack had said, it felt no different than standing in the hallway, except that everything was warped by the wavy, blue light. Michael stopped at the far end of the tunnel, at the exit of the wormhole.

Kate looked back from the way they had come. The computer generated hallway was visible though rippling.

"Here goes nothin'," Michael said.

Kate turned back in time to see Michael step out.

"Come on," he said. "It's no problem."

Kate had stopped breathing. "Here goes nothin'" echoed in her head, and she stepped through into a small closet built of stone. The wormhole closed and the computer generated hallway disappeared. The undulating distortion was gone, leaving only the stone wall. She pressed the red button on her wristband and the wormhole reappeared.

"Just like Rudy said." She let go of the button and the wormhole closed again.

Michael took off his headgear. So did Kate.

"What are we going to do with these?" she asked.

"I don't know. Let's check out the barn."

"Hoping that 'little something' Rudy mentioned is a horse?"

"Yeah." Michael stretched the word nearly to two syllables. He peered out of the storage room.

"Be careful," Kate said.

"There's nobody around. Come on."

Weeds sprouted on the path to the barn. Its big, double doors, stood wide open. The pungent aroma of old hay and manure was evident but not overpowering. But the smell was definitely horse.

The barn had a broad central corridor with four stalls on each side.

Michael ran from one to the next. Kate wandered down the corridor.

Beyond the last stalls, the corridor opened to a large area with a hay loft above. At the end was another set of doors.

"They're all empty," Michael called.

"Hey, look at this," Kate said. Clothing was stacked at the foot of the ladder that led up to the loft. "A pair of pants, a skirt—two shirts, two blankets, and—two pairs of boots."

"I guess that's what Rudy meant. We're not dressed right," Michael said.

They were wearing tee shirts and jeans. How was that going to look to—anyone they might meet?

"Your shirt's gonna stand out," Kate said. It was plain grey, but had the Nike "swoosh" prominently displayed.

"I'll probably be lookin' like a billboard. Except they probably don't even have billboards."

He lifted an old blue shirt, rough as burlap, and pulled it over his head. The shirt was long. Fringed at each elbow and wrist. It had no collar, just a slit at the neck with leather lacing.

"This will work," he said. "Your shirt's okay. No designs on it."

"Yeah but people will probably think it's underwear." Kate fingered the fine fabric of a bone white shirt. Ruffled front with buttons at the neck and a small collar. Cuffed sleeves. She pulled it on. Then she lifted the skirt by its waist band. Long, sky blue with pleats. Ties at the back of the waist. Wide at the bottom. Pretty, in an old-fashioned way. "Did girls wear pants in 1778?"

"Doubt it."

Kate stepped into the skirt, pulled it over her jeans and tied the strings in the back. She stretched out her foot, toe to the floor. The skirt covered her jeans. But what about her cross trainers? "You gonna change shoes?"

Michael looked at his feet. He was wearing his high-top riding shoes. Looked like basketball shoes with a heel.

"My shoes are screaming 'look at me, I'm an alien.'" They weren't neon beacons like some kids wore, but they weren't exactly subtle, either. He picked up a worn out, old boot and looked it over. It was ankle length with rawhide laces. The leather was cracked, frayed and tired. He squinted. "I think I'll keep mine."

The tattered boots looked none too attractive to Kate, either. Who had been wearing these things?

A square leather knapsack hung by its shoulder strap on the barn wall. Kate lifted it from its hook. Even empty it was heavy.

"We can pack our virtual reality gear in here," Kate said.

"Might as well pack this other stuff, too—just in case." Michael handed her the blankets, pants and boots.

"Aren't you gonna at least change pants?"

"My jeans will be okay. They're almost the same color as this shirt. Don't you think?"

Kate didn't think so. "Do you really want to take the chance of being noticed?"

Michael held up the pants. No zipper, no buttons. Just a string around the waist. "I guess not. Turn around."

"Okay." Kate packed the blankets and their gear. "This won't all fit in here. It's now or never for the boots."

"I'm sticking with my own shoes," Michael said.

"What if they make you suspicious?"

"Then I'll deal with it," Michael said.

Kate looked at the short, ratty boots. Anything to avoid being noticed. She took off her cross trainers and laced up the old boots. Kind of snug, but not too bad.

"Let's check out the house," Michael said.

Kate tossed her cross trainers and the other boots into the corner under the loft.

"You want me to take the pack?"

"That's okay." Kate slung the knapsack over her shoulder.

They headed for the doors. Kate followed Michael down the path toward the storage room on the side of the house. The house was stone, mostly grey and white. All odd shapes and sizes. But somehow this jumble of odd stones had been fashioned into straight walls and true corners. The side had a single, shuttered window divided into small panes, most of which were broken, leaving jagged fangs of glass in the frame.

The front of the farmhouse was shaded by a small porch, rotted and sagging. They tiptoed up three rickety steps. The door was ajar. It was deathly quiet. Michael pushed the door open. The hinges groaned. They stepped into the darkness. The only light beamed through cracks in the ceiling, gilding countless airborne flecks of dust.

The space was wide open, but the remnants of walls showed the house had once had a few rooms. A tall stone fireplace, blackened by years of soot, dominated one wall. The house didn't have a single stick of furniture.

"Now what?" Kate felt a little jittery about being inside. But she felt the same about going outside.

"Somehow we've got to locate Lafayette."

Kate took a last look around, then followed Michael into the sunshine.

four

The air was heavy with humidity and pollen. The day was hot.

A single path led away from the house, a trail of two parallel ruts. Michael and Kate followed it into a grassy meadow.

Michael's eyes panned the surroundings for any movement. There was nothing but the sway of grass in the breeze. He strained to hear any sound. Nothing but the twittering of birds.

His thoughts raced. How could Mack do this to them? No way could they possibly be ready for anything that

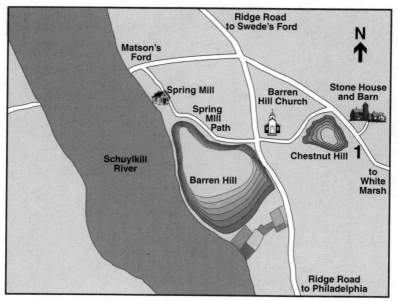

1   Michael and Kate meet Gimat

might happen. This trail would end somewhere. Then what? Would there be someone to ask? What would they do when they met someone?

"What are we going to do when we reach the road?" Kate asked.

"What road?"

"Well, these ruts must be from wagon wheels. The farmer, or whoever, probably drove his wagon to market or town or somewhere."

"So maybe we'll run into somebody who knows where Lafayette is," Michael said.

"Or maybe we'll run into bad guys first. How would we even know the difference?"

Why hadn't they asked Mack more questions? It was so stupid.

"You ever heard of Lafayette?" Kate asked.

"Yeah, but heard of him is about it. And we don't know anything about John."

"We know some things. He was a private in the cavalry. He's with Lafayette. And he's got a great family."

"You, know, I had no idea my family fought in the Revolution. I always figured my ancestors were slaves." Michael was stopped by his own words. "People will think I'm a slave."

"I hadn't thought of that."

Why would she? Michael was the one who would have to deal with it. And with Rudy and wormholes and all, he hadn't even thought of it. "I can't believe I didn't realize it before."

At the edge of the meadow, the trail entered the forest. Dark woods crept right to the path's edge.

They had walked a few yards into the woods when Kate stopped.

"This is freaking me out. It's too dark and spooky in here."

"It's better 'cause we're not out in the open. Anyway, we've got to go. Come on."

The trees on both sides of the trail were tangled into a thicket through which no light penetrated. Boughs of the nearest trees reached right to the ground, so thick with leaves that their trunks were shrouded from view.

"When we meet someone, I'll probably be arrested for being a runaway. You'll have to say that I'm your slave and we're headed somewhere."

"Michael, I can't do that."

"You'll have to. We got no choice. It'll be all right. We're just acting. Just playing a part."

Now and then, a cloud drifted across the sun, throwing shadows that lingered, then yielded to the light.

"Michael, I keep seeing something move out of the corner of my eye."

"Where?"

"Both sides. Everywhere."

"Come on." Michael ducked off the path into the thick growth of trees. Kate followed. "Stay quiet. We'll watch for a while and see what's up."

After a few minutes, Michael was getting impatient. "See anything?"

"No."

"It was probably just the shadows from the clouds playing tricks on you. Let's go."

After about a mile, the path opened onto a dirt road, clearly more well traveled.

"Which way now?"

"I don't know," Michael said, "but we've gotta be careful. How come there's no signs of life?" He had been happy about it at first. Now it was eerie. "No one on the road. No farmers, no animals. Nothing."

"Yeah, it's spooky. Like the whole area is abandoned."

"Abandoned, like in a war zone."

In the quiet, Michael heard the hoof beat of horses. "Wait. Hear that?" They were close and coming fast! "Hide!" Michael said.

He lunged for the right edge of the road. Kate started for the left. The hoof beats were louder. Michael jumped into the thicket and turned to look back.

Kate had stopped in the middle of the road. Then she took a step toward the right. Then stopped. She reversed again, like a squirrel before an oncoming car.

The hoof beats were crashing, impossibly loud.

The sound seemed to shake her from indecision. She charged toward Michael.

Two galloping horses rounded the corner from behind the line of trees. The riders pulled up hard. The big animals dug in with their hind legs and, with forelegs straight, pounded the road into dust. Kate recoiled. The horses stopped on either side of her, blocking both ways to the woods.

One rider wore a long coat with a frilly front and brass buttons. His pants looked like tights and he wore high boots. A showy feather plume topped his tall cap. He sat straight in the saddle. The other's clothes were plainer and he wore a three cornered hat.

Obviously in the military. But which military?

"You should not be out here unescorted, young miss," the fancy soldier said in a strong French accent. "From where have you come?"

"A house just down the road," Kate said.

"I didn't know any of these houses were still occupied," the man said. "Where are you going?"

"Away. From the trouble."

"On foot? Where do you hope to get?"

Michael stepped from the thicket. Both men pulled muskets from saddle holsters and pointed them at Michael.

"We're looking for General Lafayette," Michael said.

"Your slave?" he asked Kate.

"No," Kate gasped.

"Yes," Michael said. "Her slave. I'm trying to get her somewhere safe. And we need to find the General."

"For what do you need to see General Lafayette?"

"We have information for him."

He kept the musket trained on Michael. "I am Major Gimat, the General's aide. You may tell me your information."

"The British are planning to trap the General," Michael said.

"Yes? What are the details?"

"The details?"

"Yes. The details. Where, when, how?" He seemed then to notice Michael's shoes. "You're no slave. Those boots are not the footgear of a slave. The young lady says 'no', and you say 'yes'. And you do not speak like a slave. You pretend to have information, but you have no details. I think you are trying to find out where our camp is—for the British. Bumbling loyalist spies."

"No," Kate said, "really, we're not."

"Militia," the other man said, gesturing to two riders coming slowly down the road from the other direction.

These two riders were raggedly dressed. They seemed not to wear uniforms at all. And they were in no rush.

"Gentlemen, I am Major Gimat from General Lafayette's camp."

"We're with the Virginia Militia. On our way to the General with a letter. Are we headed right?"

"Yes. In about a half mile," Gimat pointed back from the way he had come, "this road will be joined by a smaller road. Our camp is another three or four miles down that road at Barren Hill. I was on my way to speak with your General Potter when I came across these two. I believe it possible they are British spies." Gesturing toward Michael, Gimat said to his companion, "Assure that he is unarmed and search her knapsack."

The Continental soldier patted Michael down and took the knapsack from Kate. Michael tried to appear indifferent when the soldier opened it. Interest would arouse suspicion. Maybe Kate put the gear on the bottom. Maybe the guy wouldn't rummage beyond the blankets.

The soldier pulled the blankets out and dropped them on the ground. Then he pulled out a handful of virtual reality gear and held it aloft. "Look here."

"Let me have that," Gimat said. To Kate, he said, "What is this?"

"Just female things," Kate said.

She's thinking quickly, hoping the mysteries of "female things" would end the question.

"I don't think so," Gimat said.

To the militiamen, he said, "I want you to take these two and this paraphernalia to General Lafayette with this warning. These two are possibly British spies. We must hold them as a precaution. Do you understand?"

"Yes, Major."

"I must proceed with my mission. Tell General Lafayette I will explain my suspicions when I return."

"Yes, sir."

Gimat and his companion rode off.

The ragged militiamen's posture slumped.

"Get those blankets and stuff them back in the bag," one said. "Then give it to me."

Michael pretended to help Kate with the blankets. "Are you okay?"

"Yeah, but I really screwed up," she said.

"My shoes didn't help," he whispered.

"Come on, come on," the militiaman said.

Kate handed him the knapsack. He added the virtual reality gear.

"Now get walking."

Kate and Michael walked down the road with the two horses following closely behind and guns pointed at their backs.

"At least this way, we'll find Lafayette," Michael said.

"But how will we get our gear back?"

"I don't know."

How would they explain to Lafayette? Just say, hey, General, we're from the future and that's our time travel stuff. Probably have better luck with that female mystery stuff.

The militiamen were talking, too.

"These two are slowing us down too much, George."

"General Potter won't like it."

"We could be free of them, you know."

"What do you mean, Henry?"

Michael went cold. What did Henry mean?

"We could just march them into a field and be on our way. After all a lot of our boys have died because of spies."

"He said they 'might' be spies."

"He said, 'possibly'. That's the fancy officer way of saying they are."

Was Kate catching this? He stole a glance her way. She glanced back. No question.

"But when that Major comes back, he'll be looking for them," George said.

"We'll just say they attacked us and we had to shoot them."

"You want to claim they attacked us? A girl and her slave boy?"

"Well then, we'll say they started to run and we couldn't take any chances. We'll give the gear to General Lafayette and that will end it. No one will worry about a couple of spies. We'll do it at the first clearing we come to. These woods must end somewhere."

"We've got to do something," Michael whispered.

"If we run, we'll make their story true," Kate said.

"If there's any distraction, break for the woods. Just don't hesitate," Michael said.

They walked for a long time. No distraction presented itself. And no clearing.

"These woods will never clear, George. We should end it right here on the road."

"I've been thinking it over, Henry. It's not right. They might not be spies. We should deliver them the way Major Gimat said."

At first, Michael and Kate didn't realize the horsemen had stopped to argue. They kept walking.

"You're going to cross me, aren't you? You goody-two shoes cowheart," Henry yelled.

"It's not that I'm scared. It's just wrong. That's all, plain wrong," George said.

Maybe they wouldn't notice. Michael and Kate kept walking. They opened up a forty or fifty foot lead on the stalled horsemen.

"Halt!" one of them yelled.

"Now!" Michael bolted for the woods. This time Kate broke the same direction, without hesitating. A shot cracked, so loud it seemed to rip the air, and something thudded into the ground just behind them. Michael hurtled into the thicket. He was running blindly, unable to see the ground the leaves were so thick. After a few strides, he found himself floating for a moment, then he crashed down into the bottom of a four foot deep pit. Kate jumped in next to him. When Michael gathered his wits, he saw they were in a bowl shaped hole about eight feet across. The bottom was mud. The foliage was so thick around the pit, it made it invisible.

The militiamen were yelling.

"It's okay," Michael whispered, "it's too thick for horses and they won't dismount to chase us. We're home free."

But the voices grew closer. Michael lifted his finger to his lips. The two men had dismounted and were searching through the undergrowth. He could hear footsteps and the rustling of leaves. The footsteps got closer. A shoe protruded through the leaves and paused on the very edge of their pit. Michael held his breath.

"Henry," the man yelled.

Michael's heartbeat seemed so loud, he half expected the man to hear it. Kate squeezed his hand. Hard.

One more step and the guy would fall into the pit with them.

"Henry," he called again.

"Over here, George."

George stepped this way and that, apparently unaware he was on a precipice and only a few feet from them. Then he moved away.

Michael and Kate lay in the mud in complete silence.

"Now you've done it, you chucklehead. We've lost them."

"You've no call to roast me about it. If we'd been doing as we were ordered, none of this would have happened."

"So you're saying it's my fault? That's rich."

"I'm saying we should get out of here before our horses are lost, too. Or we're visited by Tories."

The militiamen kept bickering as they walked away. Even when they were too far for Michael to make out much, he could still hear Henry occasionally yell an insult. "Saphead," then "rattlebrain," then even the put-downs were inaudible. They were probably back on the road.

Michael and Kate didn't move for a long time after the sound of hoof beats retreated into the distance. They just sat in the boggy pit, in the reeking loamy soil and rotting leaves.

The longer it was silent, the more confident Michael felt of their safety. He motioned to Kate and they crawled out of their den to the edge of the road. Michael hoped to see the discarded knapsack with their gear. He peeked through the leaves. No militia-men. But there in the middle of the road was the knap-sack and a pile of blankets.

They dragged through the thicket back onto the roadway and ran to the knapsack. Michael lifted it and peered inside. Shaking his head, he turned the knapsack upside down and shook it. Nothing. No gear. No way home.

"We're off to a pretty good start," Michael said. "Already been arrested, robbed and almost killed."

"It's all my fault. If only I had gotten off the road."

"Don't be taking all the credit. You're not the only chucklehead." He smiled crookedly. "If I had changed my shoes they might have bought our story."

"And I messed up our story even though we talked about you pretending to be . . . "

"You've got to say it, Kate—your slave. Better get used to it."

"Sorry, Michael."

"Don't bust yourself up about it. Hey, at least we found out where Lafayette is."

Kate appreciated Michael's encouragement, but still she felt she had buckled under pressure. Like she always did. She had come to expect it of herself. She looked down at her sky blue dress and white blouse, soggy and streaked with mud. The sorry, droopy sight matched her self-image.

Michael said something. She hadn't heard him.

"What'd you say?"

"It's gonna be dark soon. We can't make it to Lafayette. We'd never find the way in the dark. But we gotta get off the road."

"We can go back to the house," Kate said.

Michael nodded. "And start in the morning."

They stuffed the blankets into the knapsack.

As dusk approached, they backtracked toward the old farmhouse. They stuck close to one side of the road, for quick access to the woods should anyone come by. Kate eyed the woods nervously. The darker it got, the faster they walked.

"Michael, what are we going to do without that gear?"

"We'll get it back."

"From those two fools?"

"No. But they're worried about getting into trouble. You heard them," Michael said.

"Yeah."

"And if Major Gimat gets back and finds out they haven't given the gear to Lafayette, they'll get hammered. So they'll make up some story about how we got away and they'll give the gear to the General."

"Then all we have to do is get it back from Lafayette," Kate said. "Any ideas?"

"Not yet. First we have to get in to see him. But at least we know where to go."

As they got closer, the little house and barn began taking shape in the fading light.

"It feels a little like coming home," Kate said. But her feelings changed as they approached. The slumping porch roof seemed like a furrowed brow disapproving of them. Loose shutters catching the breeze clacked against the house.

The front door was still open. Inside it was even darker. No light beamed through cracks in the ceiling. The floor creaked as though whining about every footstep. The fireplace whispered with the draft down the chimney.

"On second thought, it doesn't seem all that much like home," Kate said.

"Yeah. It's kinda freaky. And there's nothing to sleep on in here anyway. Let's go out to the barn."

Kate was anxious to leave the house, but the barn

looked hardly more hospitable. It did have that loft, and being off the ground would be comforting. The ladder was sturdy. The loft was small, but easily big enough for the two of them. There was a generous layer of loose hay and a small window for fresh air.

It was nearly dark when Kate passed Michael one of the blankets. She nested into the hay and tried to relax.

"Hey, Kate?"

"Yeah."

"Do you wish you stayed home?"

"No. Just hoping we get back."

"Definitely. Anyway, thanks."

All light had faded. The loft was completely dark.

"What would we do if we couldn't get back?" Kate asked.

"I don't know. Where could we go? How could we earn money? I don't even know what the old money looks like, or even if they call their money dollars and cents."

"I don't either. I've got some money, but it probably won't be any good."

"The big one for me is, would I have to have proof that I'm free?"

"Proof?"

"Yeah, like a paper that says I'm not a slave."

"Aren't we going to say that you're—my—slave?"

"Yeah, at first. But if we save John and Lafayette, then what? We can't say that forever."

"Maybe they can help us figure it out."

"Will we tell them we're from the future?" asked Michael.

"They'd probably think we were crazy, or witches or something. We'd better get that gear back."

"I've got no clue what we'll tell Lafayette. But it had better be good."

Kate had no clue either. She couldn't focus on it at that moment. All she could think about was home. Her parents. Her little brother. Her room. Her friends. Swim team. Even race day seemed a pleasant thought. Thoughts of home turned into drowsy, phantom images. Finally, she fell asleep.

Sometime during the night Kate had a dream. She was on the starting block looking down into her team's pool. She leaned, sprang, stretched and plunged into the cool water. It felt like a night breeze as she glided. She could hear Coach Sanders talking to a swim meet official about her start. "She wasn't nervous on that one. That was a good start. She's breathing." The voice became a little clearer and a little louder, as though no longer muffled by the water. But it wasn't Coach Sanders's voice anymore. Little by little her sleeping mind gave way, and the voices became clearer still. She opened her eyes. She was hearing a real conversation.

In the dim, indirect moonlight she could make out Michael's sleeping shape. She reached over and touched his arm. Don't make a sound, Michael, please.

Luck was with her, he raised up silently on one elbow to listen.

"It's been ten miles. Finally a few minutes rest," said a gravelly voice.

"I'll suffer to be a little wayworn for a chance to trap that Marquis," said another man.

The two men spoke with heavy accents. And they were close, maybe just below the loft's window. In the background were sounds of other men and horses moving about.

"We'll rout those ragged beggars. I heard they're half starved, barefooted and barely armed," said a third man.

"But the French aren't."

"Maybe when we capture Lafayette, the frogs will lose their taste for the fight."

"You mean, *if* we catch him. If we can close the trap by early morning," the gravelly voice said.

"Then, hey, presto, we'll nab him still in his night clothes."

Several men laughed gruffly.

"And we'll cut them off from the river and their precious General Washington."

"Then we must not dawdle, gentlemen. Let's go. We best not keep General Grant waiting."

Shuffling. They were moving around. The barn door groaned. It was opening. Had someone seen them? Were they caught? Kate held her breath. Her stomach quaked.

"The horses will be safe in here," the gravelly voice said. A man walked across the barn, the clopping of hooves following him. A lantern's light played across the barn's walls and roof. Others came into the barn. The clopping sounds mingled. Couldn't count how many horses. Leather creaked. Sounded like they were putting horses in the stalls. The clatter of hooves stopped. The men plodded out. The light disappeared. The barn door groaned closed. All was quiet, save the idle sounds of the horses.

"Now we've got some details. We've gotta get to Lafayette," Michael whispered.

Kate nodded, then pressed a finger to her lips. She crept to the window sill and listened. She heard remote sounds. Probably men were resting in the fields. She peered out the window. She could see no one. She crawled back to Michael. "It's clear. We'd better go, if we're going."

"Three or four miles. No chance on foot," Michael said.

"But I couldn't handle one of those horses if they chased us."

"You can't stay here. They'll search the barn when they discover a horse is missing. You gotta ride with me. And we've got to go—now." Michael made soft scratching sounds as he crawled through the hay.

Okay. Gotta go now. But not without the knapsack. Leaving it would seem like giving up on the gear. Kate grabbed the knapsack and crawled to the top of the ladder gripping it as though it were a lifeline.

The feeble moonlight failed to penetrate beyond the loft. The barn below was in utter darkness, as though Kate had closed her eyes and was descending into an abyss. She couldn't even see Michael on the ladder below her but she could hear him and she felt every shake of the ladder as he scrambled down. Suddenly the shakes became a single sliding shudder ending with a crash to the floor in the darkness below.

"Michael, are you all right?"

One false step had sent Michael slipping down the ladder. Though it seemed like slow motion, he had been unable to grab the rungs as he fell. When he crashed to the floor on one knee, his shoulder and face jammed against the ladder. He tasted a little blood from the inside of his cheek.

"I'm okay," he whispered. "Don't move." He didn't know how loud his fall had been, but the horses were a little stirred up. He hoped nobody else heard. Had to wait. Had to give the horses a minute to calm down.

He would make himself count to twenty, slowly. He only made it to ten. Even that seemed forever. And the horses were settled.

"Come down slow. Wait at the bottom." Michael had barely made a sound. Had she heard him?

The ladder creaked. She must have.

In the absolute darkness of the barn, Michael could not make out a single image. Not even his own hand extended before him. He pictured the barn's layout and guessed at the course that would lead to the corner of the first stall. His mouth still smarted from that fall against the ladder and he didn't want to find the corner of the stall with his face, so he lifted his arms before him, bent at the elbow. Combination feelers and bumpers.

After seven or eight steps he still hadn't touched anything. Had he gone the wrong direction? He couldn't be lost. After all, he was surrounded by walls. He had to hit something sooner or later. But there was no time to waste. He turned to his left and took a step.

His left arm bumped into something. The straight side of the stall. Not the corner, but a start.

Running his hand against the wood, he slid to his right until he found the corner of the stall and then the front. He lifted the large iron latch. The stall door creaked. The horse stirred. He slipped into the stall and backed up to the inside of the wall. Didn't want to get crushed by a nervous horse.

"Hey, big guy. It's okay," Michael said in the most soothing whisper he could muster. He slipped to the front corner of the stall where he hoped he'd find the horse's head.

"Just coming to say hello. Not going to hurt you," he cooed. He held out his hand and felt around as he inched. Then he felt horse. Neck and shoulder. The horse shied away. Got to find one he could connect with—a little chemistry. This wasn't it. But he could give them a head start. Michael reached down and unbuckled the girth, the strap under the horse that holds on the saddle, and let it swing free.

He walked toward where the door should be, arms crossed in front.

Once outside the stall, he slid along until he came to another stall door and slipped inside. Empty.

He repeated the exercise in two more stalls. These had horses. But no chemistry. He left their girths unbuckled. This was so slow. Those guys could be back at any moment.

As he entered the fifth stall, the horse nickered, a soft puttering sound. The horse equivalent of a cat's purr and music to Michael's ears. He extended his hand and inched toward the sound. This time, when he hit "horse", it was soft velvet. Only one spot that soft, between the nostrils. The horse had turned to face him. Good sign. "Hey, boy. How you doin?"

Michael inched closer, keeping his hand on the horse's nose. The horse took his fingers gently between its floppy lips. Affection in the world of horses. "We're gonna be friends, boy."

Michael was standing in front of a tall horse. Gently touching its face with both hands, he lowered his face until they were nose to nose. The horse inhaled Michael's breath. A sign of recognition, affection and familiarity. This was the horse.

Michael clasped the reins, but with its superior night vision, the horse seemed to be leading Michael. "So you want to help, huh, big guy?" Michael whispered. He stopped in what he hoped was the middle of the barn.

"Kate?"

"Yeah."

"Got one. Come toward my voice. Check the door."

Despite the barn's total darkness, faint moonlight outlined the big double doors.

Michael could hear Kate shuffling along toward him and he reached out. Their hands touched, then she moved beyond him. Michael stroked the horse's muzzle.

Kate reached the door and paused. Then she pushed it slowly.

Michael winced with each creak of the ancient hinges.

With one hand always in contact with the horse, Michael moved to its side and set his left foot in the stirrup. The horse stood stone still. Another sign of welcome. Michael stepped up in the stirrup, swung his leg over and sat in the saddle.

After the complete darkness, the dim moonlight from the open doors seemed generous. He walked the horse back to the ladder. "Come on. Climb up," he whispered.

Kate hurried to the back of the barn. She climbed the first rungs and gathered up her skirt. Michael offered her an arm, she swung her leg over the horse and was up. She grasped Michael around the middle and held on tight.

Michael walked the horse slowly toward the open door.

It was taking forever to get out of that barn.

"Easy, big guy," Michael murmured.

The horse was incredibly quiet. Like he was tiptoeing. How could he know? Maybe reading Michael's body language. Still every noise seemed loud. They were only ten feet from the door.

"Well, gents, no rest for the weary." The voice was gruff.

"Odd, I thought we closed those doors." Another voice.

The shadows of five men appeared in the doorway.

"Go, Meadow!" Michael yelled. The horse bolted toward the open doors. The men scattered.

They galloped down the path.

In moments the others would jump onto their horses and fall as the unbuckled saddles slipped off. A moment after that, they would be up riding, saddles tightened.

"C'mon Meadow," Michael said. They rode as fast as they could away from the barn.

Would there be soldiers on the old wagon trail? Definitely. Couldn't be that lucky.

But when they turned onto the trail, there was no one. Kate bounced around, but held on tight. Michael slowed Meadow.

"How you doin' Kate? Balanced?"

"Sort of."

"Ready to go?"

"Go for it," Kate said.

Michael squeezed his legs around Meadow and they took off again.

The moonlit trail was empty. The cool night air blew in their faces. And Meadow ran.

Michael strained to hear any chase, but Meadow's hooves smothered all sound. Maybe they hadn't followed. Like it was against orders, or they had other business to attend to, or something.

Then, around the next bend, Michael's hopes had a blowout. Something had moved on the trail ahead.

Sentries," Michael said.

"What?" Kate wasn't sure what sentries were, but she knew it wasn't good.

"Up ahead."

Kate had been hunkered down against Michael's shoulder. While they galloped, she was too uncomfortable to look ahead and too afraid to look behind. Now she stretched to peer over Michael's shoulder. A chill shook her. Two men, probably lookouts, were scrambling around on the side of the road.

Michael swerved Meadow to the left, but the woods were too thick. He pulled Meadow to the right. Again, no where to go. Couldn't turn around, soldiers chasing.

"Gotta run it," Michael said. He pulled Meadow back onto the trail and they charged. But by then the sentries had moved into the trail with rifles aimed.

Michael slowed Meadow.

"Got no choice, Kate. Nowhere to go," Michael said.

"Halt in the name of the King!" one of the sentries yelled.

In the name of the King. British. Oh no.

"What have we here?" said the other, tall and thin. "A Negro boy and a white girl riding at breakneck speed in the wee hours of the morning."

The other sentry, shorter and younger, stepped closer, his musket leveled at Michael's chest.

"We're escaping the rebels," Michael said.

"Silence, boy! Let's hear from the young lady," said the shorter one, turning to Kate.

Her insides were jumping. Got to follow Michael's lead. "Our farm was overrun by rebels. We're running away—over the river and through the woods—to Grandmother's house we go." It just slipped out. Unbelievable. Would they know that old rhyme?

Their faces showed nothing.

"Not likely, young lady. That's no farm nag you're riding." The taller soldier assessed Meadow. "The saddle bears the markings of His Majesty's Dragoons. I think we've caught ourselves a pair of horse thieves.

Maybe running to warn Lafayette. Eh?" He turned to the shorter sentry. "Get an escort to take them back to General Grant."

"Yes, sir." The shorter soldier ran back down the road and disappeared into the darkness.

Kate heard hoof beats coming down the trail behind them.

"Now, blacky, give me the reins and dismount."

The soldier approached Meadow and lowered his musket to reach for the reins.

The hoof beats were getting louder and coming fast, like the approach of rolling thunder. For a moment the sentry turned, distracted by the sound.

"Now, Meadow!" Michael yelled. The horse reared and jumped sideways, knocking the soldier down and sending the musket flying. Kate hadn't been ready for that. With Meadow's front legs high off the ground, she began to slip.

Meadow whinnied and sprang into a gallop. The force of acceleration pulled Kate's legs out from under her. She was face down, legs flapping out over Meadow's tail. Her stomach pounded against Meadow's rump, knocking the wind out of her. She wanted to crumble into a ball, but she couldn't get her legs. All she could do was hold tight around Michael with fingers laced. Like a flag in the wind.

Can't fall. Won't fall. She strained. Her grip was slipping, fingers sliding apart. She grabbed two fistfuls of Michael's shirt. No good. She was going to fall.

Michael slowed Meadow. Kate's legs dropped over Meadow's rump. She let go of Michael's shirt, and as she began to slip down, he grabbed her waistband and yanked her back up. She grabbed the saddle and pulled her legs back under her, righting herself on Meadow. She forced in a deep breath to unknot her stomach.

A musket shot thundered, a shattering, cracking boom.

Meadow sprang back to a gallop.

Another musket shot seemed to tear the air. Then another. Kate held her breath, expecting to feel the blinding pain of a bullet.

She hung on tight. Meadow ran. Everything turned to slow motion. The speed, the movement, the wind in her face.

The sounds of musket shots diminished until they were mere cracks and then ceased. Michael turned to look behind, then Meadow's pace slowed.

"Are they coming?" Kate asked.

"Looks like they gave it up."

Kate unclenched herself and craned to look back. With the first light of dawn glowing behind, she would have been able to see any riders following. But there were none.

Michael slowed Meadow further. "Got to give Meadow a breather."

"Is it okay? Won't they be after us?"

"They're probably afraid of getting too close to Lafayette's camp."

"And spoiling their surprise?"

"Yeah. They're probably hoping we won't go to Lafayette. Hoping we're just ordinary horse thieves. But Meadow is no ordinary horse," Michael said.

"You've named him already?"

"It just seemed right. Hey, Kate, what's up with the 'over the river' thing?"

"Just slipped out. Sorry."

"Hey, forget it. No harm, no foul."

"Thanks for pulling me up back there."

"No prob."

"Michael, we're getting close to Lafayette. How are we going to get our stuff back?"

"Gonna have to think of something good to tell him."

"Any ideas?" Kate asked.

"Not yet. You?"

Michael picked up Meadow's pace a little.

"Well, we could tell them the truth."

"Yeah, right," Michael said. "Hey, General Lafayette, we're from the future and we need the gear to get home."

"I wasn't serious," Kate said. "How about, it's part of an invention."

"Okay, whose? And what invention?"

"I don't know. Maybe a sick relative needs it."

"Maybe it's like a voodoo, medicine man thing," Michael said. Then he pulled Meadow to a sudden stop. "Somebody's up there," he whispered.

Kate looked over his shoulder. The trees on the right side of the road receded ahead, opening a clearing in which a building stood in silhouette. Men moved about in the clearing. They seemed not to have noticed Michael and Kate.

Michael turned Meadow, walked him a few steps back up the trail, then froze.

"Halt! Who goes there?"

eight

Two men blocked their path, guns raised.

No chance to run. They must have been hiding in the trees. These guys were dressed in rags. Outlaws?

"Dismount," one said. "We'll walk you in to see the Captain."

"Are you Continentals?" Michael asked.

"No talk. Just get down."

Kate swung her leg around and slid down. Michael was next.

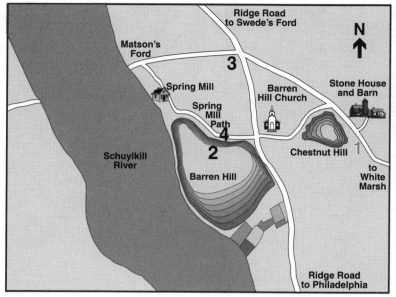

2 Camp at Barren Hill
3 British roadblock
4 Lafayette's course to Spring Mill Path

"Go on now." The man gestured in the direction of the building.

Michael and Kate walked down the road.

This was tricky. What to say? These guys probably weren't British—too ragged. Might be loyal to the British. Might not. Might just be a gang of thieves. If they were with the British, they'd get Michael and Kate as horse thieves anyway. Michael decided to take a chance.

They stopped in front of a small crowd, a shabby, motley bunch with a hard look and pointed muskets.

"Found these two on the road, about to scoot."

A man stepped forward. A big man.

"What are you about?"

"We're trying to find the Continentals," Michael said.

"You have. I'm Captain Newsome. What business have you with us?"

"We came to warn you of a British trap," Michael said.

"You were caught trying to run away. I've heard of better ways to deliver a warning."

"We didn't know you were Continentals," Michael said. "We wouldn't have been able to deliver any warning if we were caught by the British."

"True enough. Of what trap do you suppose to warn us?"

"They're going to cut you off from the river and capture General Lafayette."

"How would you know of such plans?"

"We heard them talking," Kate blurted. "When they stopped to rest."

Captain Newsome looked from Kate back to Michael. "Where did you get this horse?"

"Took him from the British. They left him in the barn. Couldn't get here in time without him."

"So you saw British soldiers in the area?" The Captain looked around.

"A few miles back," Michael said.

"This had better not be a trick."

"It's no trick, Captain," Michael said.

"Too risky to ignore," the Captain muttered. "One of my men will take you to camp. First you must be disarmed. Check for weapons!"

One man searched their knapsack, while another patted down Michael's shirt. "All clear, Captain."

"Banks!" Captain Newsome barked.

Michael jumped. Would it be John Banks?

"Here, Captain," a deep voice spoke from the darkness and a black man rode forward.

"This is Private Banks," Newsome said to Michael and Kate. "He'll escort you to camp."

Michael stared, jaw slack, as though a denizen of his dreams had just arrived.

Turning to Banks, the Captain said, "Wake everyone if you must, but get these two to the General."

"Yes, sir." Banks turned to Michael. "Follow me."

Private Banks led them slowly past the building, a stone church bounded by a rock wall. The steeple, towering above an arched doorway, was topped with a small white cross.

Beyond the church grounds, Banks led them across another road, then up a gentle slope. In moments they were galloping down the deserted road.

"My back is aching," Kate said above the rumble of hooves.

"Can't be much farther," Michael said. Kate had been hanging on back there through some hard riding.

Michael couldn't take his eyes from Private Banks's back. Ancestors. Never really cared before. But now, flesh and blood, riding just ahead. What would he be like? Simple? Superstitious? Slaves couldn't help it. They were held down. Kept ignorant. Slavery was a hard world. Always been angry about it. Kind of eats at you. Been a little ashamed, too. Never admitted that to anybody.

In several minutes, Private Banks slowed his horse to a trot and they entered a camp. Soldiers were scattered on both sides of the road. They looked like a giant had tossed them there by the handful. Some, roused from sleep, stared as Michael and Kate passed.

Banks rode to a group of four tents. Each was the size of a small room with a peaked roof with scalloped edges.

A lone figure sat in lantern light at a table set up among the tents. When the horses stopped before him, he looked up from his papers. He rose slowly and walked toward them.

The dawn light was so thin, Michael could only make out his shape, as though he were walking through a fog. He was tall and slender with broad shoulders.

Each step brought him clearer. With his last step, the fog vanished. His clothes were fancy. His long coat was decorated with brocade and brass buttons.

"Captain Newsome sent these two with news from White Marsh," Private Banks said.

"Dismount, all of you." The man motioned toward the table. They followed him.

Their gear was on the edge of the table. Just sitting there in a pile.

"Your name, mademoiselle?"

"Kate Hammond. Ah, and this is my—slave—Michael."

Kate had finally learned her lesson, but now it was all wrong. They couldn't lie to this man. Michael didn't know why, but there was something about this guy. They had to be straight with him.

"We made up the story about me being a slave so we could get here easier. I'm nobody's slave."

Lafayette looked toward Kate.

"It's true. We made it up. He's free."

"And your true name?"

"Michael Banks."

Lafayette turned toward John.

"No relation I know of, sir."

"Allow me to present myself. I am Gilbert de Lafayette. I am pleased to make your acquaintance. And please, be seated." Lafayette sat down. His hands rested on some papers. Looked like a letter.

"We're here to warn you," Michael said, pulling up a stool. He stole a glance at the gear. It was so close.

Inclining his head toward Michael, Lafayette said, "What warning have you so early this morning?"

"A British trap. They marched all night."

"Ten miles," Kate said.

"How do you know of this trap?"

"We overheard them talking," Michael said. "They stopped to rest at—the farm."

"And what is the nature of this trap?"

"They're going to cut you off from the river," Michael said.

"By early morning," Kate said.

"How did you know where to find me?"

"Yesterday we ran into your aide on the road," Michael said.

"His name?"

"Major Gimat. He said he was on his way with a message."

"And he told you where to find our camp?"

"Not exactly," Michael said. "He told a couple of militia guys who were on their way to you."

Lafayette motioned toward the virtual reality gear. "Is this equipage yours?"

"Yes," Michael said.

"Interesting. Two militiamen reported that it had belonged to two spies. And they had shot these two spies to prevent their escape. Are you those spies?"

"Well, yes and no," Michael said. "We're not spies, but that is our gear. Those guys were going to kill us just because we were slowing them down."

"But the militiamen reported that you are spies. Why shouldn't I believe them?"

"Because they're liars trying to cover their own tails. If they were telling the truth, we'd be dead, not standing here in front of you with a warning," Michael said.

In the silence, Lafayette looked into Michael's eyes and then Kate's, as though he were somehow reading them.

Lafayette's face was narrow, even a little pinched.

But his eyes were wide and clear. He looked very young. Except his hair was thinning. He wasn't handsome exactly, but he had a kind of a presence. A magnetism.

Lafayette turned to Michael and Kate. "Thank you for your efforts on my behalf, but I believe you have seen our own Fourth Continental Dragoons. I am expecting them from that direction. They wear red and you have mistaken them for British."

"No disrespect, General, but they were definitely British." Michael leaned forward, his elbows on the table. "We took their horse. Check the saddle. That's British."

Lafayette walked to Meadow and examined the saddle. "It does appear to be British. Where did you get this horse?"

"When they stopped to rest, they left their horses to go to a meeting with General Grant. We took him."

"General Grant? Hm, perhaps we should investigate. Private Banks, ride toward White Marsh and see if you can confirm this."

"Right away, sir."

"No, wait!" Michael said. "Can't you send someone else?"

"Why?" Lafayette asked.

To keep him out of harm's way was why. Couldn't say that. What to say?

"Hurry, Private Banks." Lafayette turned toward the shadows of the tents. "Corporal."

"Yes, sir." A man stepped closer.

"Awaken Generals Poor and Woodford. Have them join me immediately.

"While we wait, let me learn a little of those who come with warnings in the night. Do you have military training, Michael?"

"No."

"What is your occupation?"

"I'm—a student."

"Ah, I have heard of a school for Africans. Kate?"

"Student."

"I, too, have had that occupation. Long ago it seems. And far from here," Lafayette said.

He looked into Kate's eyes. Sadness pulled at the corners of his mouth. He fingered the edge of his letter. His eyes glistened.

"What's the matter, General?" Kate asked.

"I am reminded that my family is so far away." He looked into Michael's eyes in that searching way of his. "Why have you such concern for Private Banks? He says he is not your relation."

"He doesn't know it, but he is," Michael said.

"I believe you speak the truth, but you speak in riddles."

"The truth is complicated," Michael said, "but it's still the truth."

"Perhaps. What is this relationship of which he is unaware?"

"Distant, but important to my family."

"Distant, but close, yes? I am distant in another way from my dear wife, Adrienne." Lafayette fingered the papers on the table. "I have just found out that my infant child, Henriette, has . . . passed away. The letters come so slowly—or not at all. I didn't even know she was ill. I am here, across the great Atlantic, fighting for the liberty of a country not even my own. And now that France is in alliance, I owe it to my King to wage this war. But at what sacrifice? I am unable even to share my Adrienne's grief."

"General, we're sorry about your daughter," Kate said.

Michael looked at Kate, thankful she had said the right thing for both of them.

"Thank you." He sighed. "These things I have not been able to speak of with anyone. Perhaps your youth has opened me up too much. Please forgive me. Now," his hand moved from the letter to their gear, "what are these?"

Silence seized the moment. Michael had been unable to think of anything plausible.

"We're from the future," Kate said.

That hit Michael like a slap. What was she doing?

"The future?" Lafayette asked.

"Yes, we came in a machine that let us travel through time. And that's our gear. We need it back now, so we can go back into the future."

Lafayette smiled for a moment. Then it faded. "Enough nonsense. What is this equipage and who fashioned it?"

Who fashioned it? Fashioned. "It's not equipment at all, General. It's fashion."

"Fashion?"

"Yeah, we wear it for style," Michael said.

Lafayette picked up the gear and turned it in his hands. "To be dapper? Show me." He handed it to Michael.

Michael slipped on the head gear. "See. It's good in bright sunlight and it looks cool."

"Cool?"

"Yeah. In style, you know. Stylish."

"Yes, I know something about foolish styles. The Macaroni Club with their purple wigs and foolish clothes."

Two older men, obviously of high rank, approached the table.

"General, what is it?" one of them asked.

"These two have come with a warning about a British army on the march from White Marsh. I've sent a courier to see if we can confirm it." Lafayette led the two men into one of the tents.

"We're from the future?" Michael whispered.

"I thought if we didn't say something pretty soon, he wouldn't believe anything. It's all I could come up with. You didn't seem to have any ideas."

"Maybe he believed the fashion thing."

The sky grew lighter and the muffled sounds of dawn gave way to the banter and clanging of early morning. The sky was clear and it was already warm.

"Maybe we should just slip the gear into the knap-sack. Maybe he'll forget about it," Kate said.

"But if he doesn't . . . "

Michael's words were drowned by pounding hooves. Private Banks was back. He dismounted with a jump as Lafayette and his companions came out of the tent.

"Sir, a British column is advancing from Chestnut Hill."

"How many and how far away?" Lafayette asked.

"The column goes out of sight. Got to be thousands. About two miles from the church."

"General Poor," Lafayette said to one of the officers, "Let's give them a battle. Your Connecticut brigade will lead."

"It will be our honor, General."

"General Woodford, send couriers to Valley Forge. Notify General Washington of the British movements and request reinforcement."

Within a few minutes, the entire camp was moving. Men shouted. Wagons and cannons were moved. The army was mobilizing before their eyes in a fascinating kind of order, almost a rhythm. Their clothes were ragged, but not their discipline. And their spirits were high.

Lafayette huddled over a map with his staff. Several soldiers began taking down the tents. Two riders picked their way through the commotion of the camp.

"My couriers," Woodford said.

"General!" one of the riders shouted. They hopped

from their horses and, off balance, collided, one knocking the other to the ground.

"What news?" Lafayette asked of the one standing.

He was panting hard and talking so fast, his words were nonsense.

"Calm down, catch your breath," Woodford said.

The man took several deep breaths. "The British have cut us off from the river. We couldn't get through to Valley Forge."

"Where did you encounter the enemy?" Lafayette's calm seemed to soothe the couriers.

"North on Ridge Road—at the junction with Swede's Ford Road."

Another rider had made his way through the camp. He rode right for General Lafayette, forcing the couriers to scurry out of his way. "Sir, we captured two British dragoons."

"Explain, Captain McLane," Lafayette said.

"My pickets, including the Oneida Indians, are stationed south along Ridge Road. A detachment of British dragoons coming up the road were surprised by the Oneida. I guess the Indians had never seen British dragoons before so they took off into the woods. And I suppose the dragoons had never seen Indians before neither, 'cause they turned tail and ran. But we captured two of them. They told us the British are setting a trap. General Howe's going to attack us on the south. General Grant's command marched all night to come around the long way. They split up to come from

Chestnut Hill on the east and block us from escape to the north on Ridge Road."

"General Poor."

"Yes, General Lafayette."

"Prepare to march. We'll retreat to the north. Cannons in the lead."

"But the British have blocked Ridge Road to the north."

"Yes, but there is another way—a path along the river. It passes the Spring Mill to Matson's Ford. We'll cross the river there, having bypassed the British completely."

This guy was cool, even in the grip of a closing trap. It affected everyone. They seemed to have complete confidence in this twenty year old general.

"Private Banks!" Lafayette called.

"Yes, sir." Banks's voice resonated.

"Tell Captain Newsome that one hundred men will reinforce him. He should spread them in the woods north of the church. The British will fear they are the head of our entire force preparing to attack. He must slow down General Grant's column. Then he can follow us to the river. If he fails, all is lost. And, Banks—"

"General?"

"Come back to tell me if Grant has been stopped, whether by feint or by fight."

Banks jumped on his horse.

"Wait. What's your first name?" Michael blurted.

"It's John." He smiled a crooked smile. His eyes twinkled. "Some day, maybe, we'll get to talk about the Banks families."

"Definitely," Michael said.

John turned as his horse sprang to speed.

Michael lifted his arm to wave at John's back. Wonder swelled in Michael's chest—to know an ancestor as a young man, only a little older than himself. And John was a cavalryman, doing important work, not a slave held down to some meaningless service. But Michael's wonder was tempered. He had done no more than meet him and John was headed to an uncertain fate, leaving Michael behind. Would he ever see John again?

How did Mack think Michael was going to protect John anyway? Especially now that he was riding away. Things were definitely getting out of hand.

After John was gone, Lafayette turned to Kate and Michael. "I am indebted to you for bringing the warning. But your situation has become perilous. You must not stay with us. If we are captured, you would be treated as spies. Michael, they would sell you into slavery in the West Indies—or worse. And Kate, . . . you simply must not be caught. Your best chance is on your own.

"You must be disguised as a boy. If captured, say you are militiamen bringing a message to me that the Virginia Militia has arrived in White Marsh. Then, perhaps you won't be treated as spies. Hide deep in the woods above the river. We cannot spare another horse,

I'm sorry. I wish you great good luck. You will need it. So will we."

He turned away. "Collins! Outfit these two as militiamen. Our mademoiselle must pass as a young man. They must," he cleared his throat and smiled, "return to their company. And pass the word that a militiaman warned us of this trap."

Lafayette turned back to Michael and Kate. "Our talk has refreshed me beyond words." He took Kate's hand and bowed slightly. "Goodbye, mademoiselle." He picked up the gear and pressed it into Michael's hands. "Take this, whether fashion, time travel, or some other truth. But keep it hidden." He smiled. "Goodbye." With military snap, he turned and strode away.

Despite the urgency they faced, Michael watched Lafayette until a small crowd of officers blocked the view. There went a man whose fame had lasted more than two hundred years. Michael had never met anyone famous before. But in this man, whose presence was both commanding and engaging, it was easy to see how his exploits had captured the imagination of the nation.

Michael handed the CTS gear to Kate and hurried to Meadow to remove the heavy dragoon saddle. Kate stuffed the gear into the pack.

Collins returned with a lighter saddle and handed it to Michael.

"This is a lot like mine at home," Michael said as he placed the saddle over Meadow.

Collins returned with an armful of clothing. He

tossed a blue knit cap to Michael, then a red one to Kate. Like a long stocking cap. Kate pulled it on and tucked in her hair. The end of the cap flopped over, dangling a little cloth tassel in her face. She reset it to one side. "How do I look?"

"A fine young lad," Collins said.

"Check this out," Michael said. His cap was shorter. "Liberty or Death" was stitched into the band above his brow.

"Careful what you ask for," Kate said.

"Right—I just might get it."

"You'll have to wear these." Collins handed Kate a pair of pants and a brown burlap shirt.

Kate slipped the shirt over her blouse. Collins turned his attention to Michael. "Now, let me look at you. Your britches'll do. But those boots—those are the strangest . . . " He squinted one eye and cocked his head. "Where'd you say you're from?"

"Ah—call it the frontier."

"I don't need the britches." Kate handed them back to Collins. "I'm already wearing a pair." She reached behind her, untied the skirt, slid it down to her ankles and stepped out of it.

The squint dropped from Collin's face. His eyes went wide. His mouth hung. Distracted from Michael's shoes, he was speechless.

Kate tossed him the skirt. "You better hold that for me. It wouldn't do for a militiaman to have a skirt in his pack."

Michael climbed into the saddle and offered his arm. Kate hooked it with hers and jumped up on Meadow. She was getting pretty good at it. And it was easier without the bunched up skirt.

"Which way?" Michael asked.

"Ah . . . " Collins closed his mouth and shook his head as if to clear a haze. "Head west across the broad top of Barren Hill." Collins pointed across the camp. "When you see the river down below, turn north to the highest point of the hill. That's your spot. You can see everywhere from there, up and down the river and across the hill. And take these." Collins handed two pistols to Michael. "You may need them. Careful, they're loaded."

"I don't know how to fire these."

"Just pull that hammer back there until it locks, then pull the trigger. No time to teach you how to reload."

"One shot?"

Collins's squint returned. "Of course. What else?"

Michael tucked them into holsters on each side of the saddle.

"Thanks for everything, man. And good luck," Michael said.

"Good luck to you." Collins turned and ran to join the camp commotion.

They rode west across the camp. One hundred soldiers headed in the opposite direction, marching in quick step. Michael's eye roved to the black soldiers, here and there, in the company. But the closest soldiers drew his attention. He studied their faces as they went by. One held a stern, cold stare. Another, nervous and flitting eyes. Most were deadpan, unreadable. In moments, they had passed.

"One hundred isn't much," Michael said. "They'll be swallowed up."

"And that plan to fool the British. That'll never work."

"Yeah, it seems a little weak. And John's gonna be right there. We can't just sit on that hilltop and wait while John gets killed or something."

"But even if we follow him, what can we do?"

"I don't know yet. But guaranteed we can't do anything from up there."

"Okay, let's go," Kate said.

Michael turned Meadow and they headed toward the church and away from the safety of the hilltop perch.

nine

Almost immediately they caught up with the one hundred soldiers, now four abreast and keeping a fast pace. Michael had to ride Meadow off the road to stay out of their way. The men panted from the steady exertion. Their leathers creaked. The pounding and shuffling of their feet raised a choking dust.

Most took no notice as Meadow glided by them. A few gave sideward glances. They were each so different, the tall, the short, the black, the white. Yet they shared something—a vibe—that made them seem all the same. In it together. All business. Hard looks. Not

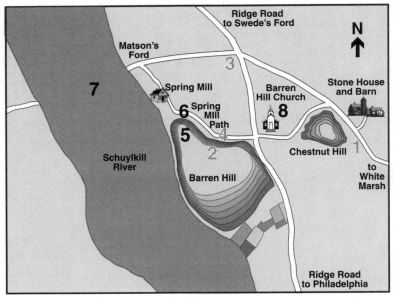

5   Bluff
6   Meadow's hiding place
7   Lafayette's army fords the river
8   Newsome's trick

directed at Kate, but hard because that's what it takes. Kate could feel a collective tension emanating from them.

In a few moments Meadow had passed them. The air cleared of dust but not of tension. Kate could see the church, tiny in the distance. She pictured its courtyard at the crossroads, surrounded by dense woods. What would Captain Newsome do to stop an army of thousands? Lafayette had said something about pretending to be a whole army. How would he do that? Kate had a bad feeling about it. And about their heading into it. What could they possibly do to protect John? He'd be ordered around. What could they do, convince Captain Newsome not to send him into danger? Yeah, right. And in the heat of battle they couldn't exactly follow him around. To do what? Jump in the way when the shooting started? Was Michael willing to stop a bullet to save John? He would be saving his own father and brother. But Mack had said Michael couldn't make it without her. What could she do to protect John and Michael? What would she do? She pressed the bottom of the knapsack. She felt the gear through the heavy material.

As the hill flattened and they closed in on the church, Michael slowed Meadow.

"What are we gonna do?" Kate asked.

"First, we've got to find John. After that, I'm not sure."

The sentries were clearing the churchyard of their gear. Michael directed Meadow through a gateway in the low stone wall surrounding the yard.

"Got a message for Captain Newsome," he shouted to one of the sentries.

"Inside," the man motioned toward the church.

Kate slid off Meadow and followed Michael through the arched front doors.

Captain Newsome was huddled with several officers.

"Captain, we have a message from General Lafayette for Private Banks," Michael said as he approached the group.

Captain Newsome looked up at Michael, then at Kate. "He sent you two here?"

"Yes, Captain. No other horses to spare."

Newsome shook his head. "Well, let's have it then."

"The message is for Private Banks."

"He's out back." Newsome gestured to a door behind the altar, then looked away, resuming his conference.

Michael and Kate found John in the yard, checking his saddle and equipment.

"What are you doing here? This is no place for you."

"I never got to tell you," Michael said, "we are related."

"How's that?"

"I'm not exactly sure, but I know you are related to my father."

"That's fine. And I'm interested in family, believe me. But you two have got to get out of here before the shooting starts."

"I can't go and just leave you here," Michael said.

"Why not? I'm supposed to be here. You're not."

"I've got to stay and help you. Make sure nothing happens."

John's forehead crinkled. "Look, son. Nothing will happen to me. Today I'm a courier. Not much chance I'll be here for the fighting. I've got to ride a message to the General as to whether or not the British are fooled."

"I'm going with you," Michael said.

"You can't do that."

"Why not?"

"You'd be leaving Kate here without a horse. That won't do. Look, when I ride back to the General, I'll be shielded by the depths of the forest. Only one thing would make my job more dangerous—that's if you tried to ride with me. There's just no sense in it."

Captain Newsome stepped from the church. "Have you given the Private his message?"

"Yes, Captain," Michael said.

"Good. Private Banks here told me that your warning saved us from a trap. And now you have brought a message from the General. You have performed a great service. Now you must find a safe place as far from this church as you can. Go with our thanks and good wishes."

Michael hesitated, as though there was something else he wanted to say.

"Go *now*." Newsome raised his hand in salute.

John nodded his approval and gripped Michael's shoulder. "You got to."

"Take care," Michael said.

"And you," John said.

Michael and Kate found Meadow waiting in front of the church. They mounted and headed up the hill.

They came again upon the one hundred soldiers. This time several seemed to look at them hopefully, as though Michael and Kate might have news that their mission was unnecessary. Some looked frightened. But as Michael rode Meadow by without a word, all faces turned back toward the church and their task.

In several minutes, Michael and Kate reached what had been Lafayette's camp so short a time before. Now it was abandoned, the last of the Continental line already distant.

As Michael and Kate left the campsite behind, Barren Hill rose in a series of inclines and flats like a huge, rough hewn stairway.

"Damn, I should've stayed," Michael said. "But I'm riding away. Just to wait up on some useless hilltop. No different than if I stayed in my room. What's the point? I needed to stay."

"But John said it didn't make any sense."

"Yeah, and I had nothing I could say."

"Because of me?"

Michael didn't answer.

"Like if I wasn't here, you could've stayed?"

Michael said nothing.

What was he mad about? None of this was her fault. Mack said she had to come. *Both of you.* It wasn't like she had even wanted to.

Kate felt a distance growing between them, unlike anything she had felt before in all the years they had been neighbors and friends.

They rode in silence for a long time until they reached the slope down to the river. It was steep, nearly a cliff. Meadow danced inches from the brink.

"He won't slip, will he?" Kate asked.

"No way," Michael said. He held Meadow dancing along the edge.

Kate hated being on the edge. Meadow could control his hooves, Michael could control Meadow. But

Kate couldn't control anything. She felt like baggage dangled out of a high rise window. Her chest was too tight to breathe. The same feeling she had leaning over the platform before her race.

"Michael, please!"

Michael pulled Meadow away from the ledge.

"You mad at me?" Kate asked.

"No."

Kate didn't believe him. "Because it's not my fault that I'm even here. I came to help. Remember?"

"Yeah. I'm just having trouble dealing with it."

"With my being here?"

"It's that I can't help. Like I'm failing my family. And maybe if you weren't—maybe if I was alone, I could have gone with John."

"But Mack said I had to be here. That you'd have no chance alone. That's just the way it is. And I didn't make it that way."

"I know it's not your fault. I should be thanking you. Sorry."

"That's okay." The distance between them was vanishing. "Maybe there's some way you can help from up here."

"Maybe. It's been a long ride. How you doin'?"

"Fine—I think." Kate groaned in mock discomfort.

"We still gotta get up there." Michael pointed north. "It's not much farther."

"I'm fine, really." Better now that they had cleared the air.

Meadow turned right and they continued up a slight grade. The river rambled way below on their left. The pitch leveled as they reached the summit, a triangular bluff jutting above the river canyon and affording them a river view to infinity.

Looking the other way a full panorama of Barren Hill sprawled before them. East, beyond sloping forest to the church. Southeast, beyond the broad hilltop to distant farms.

"That must be the Spring Mill." Kate pointed to a cluster of buildings far to the north along the riverbank.

"And those guys are really haulin'," Michael said.

The head of Lafayette's column had already reached the mill.

"Whoa, Meadow." Michael drew in on the reins.

Kate swung her right leg around and slid on her stomach down Meadow's hip and flank until her feet hit the ground. Her legs were a little wobbly and stiff.

Michael hopped down.

"We've gotta take care of business. Got to hide Meadow," Michael said.

"Where are you gonna hide him?"

"Maybe down there." Michael gestured to the side of the bluff away from the river. It was not nearly as steep on that side. "I'll check it out." He patted Meadow, walked to the crest of the bluff and stepped over.

"Don't be long, okay?"

"Yeah."

In a few steps Michael descended enough that only

his head was visible above the crest. He turned back to Kate. "Be right back, okay?"

She nodded.

One more step and he disappeared altogether behind the ridge.

Kate stamped her feet to bring back the feeling in her legs, then settled on the edge of a flat boulder, the size of a two-seat convertible. She shaded her eyes with her hand. The far-off churchyard was filled with Captain Newsome's reinforcements. But no horses. Where was John?

Michael jogged back over the ridge. "Found a great place. Come on, I'll show you." He grabbed Meadow's reins and led them, single file, over the rim.

The trees were sparse for only a few yards, then became dense. Michael improvised a roundabout path through the thicket. The further downhill they went, the thicker the woods became. Branches and leaves engulfed them, blocking the sky.

Michael stopped. And Meadow in turn. Then Kate. She could see only leaves, branches and Meadow's wide rump.

"Could you help me up here?" Michael asked.

"Sure." Kate called. But she was cornered by the snagging forest bramble on both sides and an unyielding wall of horse in the middle. Well, thorny and scratchy were inconvenient, but sinewy and titanic were impossible. So she fought through the grasping branches to Michael.

"What's up?"

"Could you hold back some of these branches so I can lead Meadow through? It's getting so thick."

"No problem."

Kate held back branches until Meadow passed. Michael waited while Kate fought ahead to do it again. The branches snagged everything, her shirt, her knapsack. Even her militia cap was snared right off her head.

Then, without warning, they went from deep shade to sunlight in a single step. They stood in a small clearing on a carpet of grass with a window to the sky, framed by treetops.

"See? Meadow can graze while we're up above," Michael said.

"And we can hide down here, too."

"If we need to. It's perfect."

Michael removed Meadow's bridle and hung it on a branch. "Stay here, big guy."

Meadow nickered, then tore a mouthful of grass.

"That means we're dismissed," Michael said. "Let's go."

They ducked back into the shade and zigzagged up hill. When they cleared the woods and topped the rim, Kate headed for the big rock. She sat in the same spot and took a deep breath. She slipped off the knapsack and felt inside for the gear. Still there. What had Lafayette really thought about it? Some other truth?

Kate scanned the distances. The only movement was Lafayette's troops trekking down the Spring Mill path.

He was so young to be leading all those soldiers. Life and death. And they followed him.

It looked now like the first part of their mission was accomplished. Lafayette wouldn't be captured. But what if they were captured. Michael, sold into slavery . . . And Lafayette couldn't even bring himself to talk about what would happen if she were caught. And the wormhole would close for good after noon tomorrow. They'd be stuck in 1778. No family. No home. No one. Nothing. Unthinkable. Jitters radiated through her arms and legs.

"We've got to be ready," Michael said. "Want to hold one of these?"

He held out one of the old pistols. Beautiful, even graceful. Carved of dark wood and polished to a patina by the touch of a thousand calloused hands. Brass fittings shined against the dark wood.

"No thanks." Kate barely budged out the words. Her voice was thin.

Michael leaned against the boulder and laid the pistols on the ground beside him. His eyebrows wrinkled. "What is it, Kate?"

"I feel so stupid. I can't catch my breath. Can't get a grip. When I'm gonna swim a race, I get stuck on 'why me?' I imagine escaping. Just stepping off the blocks—walking away. Quitting."

"But you don't."

"I did last time. I let everybody down. I don't want to quit this, though. Got to see it through."

Michael stood and faced her. He put a hand on each of her shoulders. Her jitters quieted, as though calmness could pass through him. "Kate, I forgot for a while that Mack said I couldn't do this without you. Sorry I was a jerk." Michael smiled.

"It's not that."

"What then?"

"I was thinking about getting captured. Getting stuck here."

"Yeah, I know. It's scary. But we'll be all right. Whatever happens, though, thanks for coming."

Kate breathed deeply. She half-smiled. "Yeah."

Michael leaned back against the boulder.

Kate needed conversation. "How's Meadow?" Her voice was low.

"Fine. I told him to stay quiet. He seemed to understand."

"He seems to understand everything."

"Yeah. Incredible. And he'd do anything for us."

"For *us*?"

"Definitely. You could ride him. He'd make sure of it."

Cracks sounded in the distance.

"Musket fire." Michael jumped to his feet. "At the church. Soldiers are down."

Kate could barely make them out. Motionless bodies in the churchyard. The rest of the Continentals marched around in the woods trying to look and sound like the entire army.

The British column was so long it disappeared on

the horizon. But the head of the column had stopped!

"It's working. They fooled 'em," Michael said. He pumped his fist in the air.

"You think they could see us?" Kate asked.

"Maybe."

They sidled around to the other side of the boulder and leaned on it, so they could just see over the top.

Kate looked down toward Lafayette's column. "Do you think they'll make it to the ford?"

"Some of them will."

"Is John one of them lying in the churchyard?" Kate asked. If he were, they had already failed the second part of their mission. Would Michael disappear? Leave her there alone? The image of John crumpled and life-less seemed to remove her from the here and now. She felt hollow.

"No! He's there." Michael pointed to a lone rider speeding from the church along the Spring Mill path.

An eerie silence settled over the church. The front of the British column had spread out.

"I never thought that trick would work," Michael said. "The redcoats are too chicken to check it out. A whole army being fooled by a hundred guys. I'd like to see Lafayette's face when John tells him it worked."

At full gallop, John closed quickly on Lafayette's army. He slowed as he mingled with the tail of the col-umn, and then disappeared among the mass.

The panorama was still again, except for Lafayette's steady progress, until the lone rider re-emerged from the end of the column and headed back up the Spring Mill path. When John neared the church grounds, he veered into the woods.

"He's going back to Captain Newsome," Michael said. "I better make sure Meadow's ready. I'll be right back." Michael dashed over the crest and into the woods.

Ready for what? What was Michael thinking?

In a few minutes, Newsome's men were on the march, or rather, on the run, following Lafayette's path to the ford. A single horseman, Newsome, rode with them. But where was John?

Michael jogged back over the crest. "Meadow's ready. What's up?"

"John must have given Newsome the word. They've left the church."

"I didn't hear any shots."

"Haven't been any. I don't think the British know they're gone," Kate said.

"They're about to find out."

Red-coated scouts were slinking across the church-yard. Soon they would enter the woods and find it deserted.

Newsome's Continentals raced toward Spring Mill. Kate imagined the creaking of their leathers. They were breathing the dust raised by their own pounding feet. She could almost taste it. Their faces echoed in her memory. They must be afraid, waiting for the sound of dragoons riding down on them.

The churchyard filled with redcoats. And on the road

next to the church, red horsemen began to gather.

"Where is he?" Kate couldn't find John anywhere. He wasn't among the escaping soldiers. "He can't still be at the church."

"Maybe he's already gone with another message."

Lafayette's troops had finished the river crossing and were setting up cannons on the far bank.

Newsome's group ran up the Spring Mill path, but the charging dragoons closed in fast.

"It's like they're hardly moving," Kate said, watching Newsome's foot soldiers.

"It's gonna be close." Michael began pacing back and forth behind the boulder.

Newsome rode from the back of his line to the front and back again, exhorting the men to go faster. They reached the riverbank running. The first man splashed into the river. But he lost his footing. He struggled. The stiff current was sweeping him away. Newsome drove his horse, high stepping, into the river. The soldier flailed at the saddle but slipped down into the water. He flailed again. This time he grabbed it and the horse dragged him back to solid footing. A fellow clasped his hand.

The dragoons were bearing down.

The soldiers ventured into the river in a single file, hand in hand, to avoid the current's pull. Chest deep, they bobbed in the rushing water like corks on a string. All were in, except for a dozen and their captain.

"What's he doing? Why doesn't he get out of there?" Kate felt panic.

"He's positioning those last guys to take the charge. A rear guard," Michael said.

"But there's no cover."

"No. Nowhere to hide."

The rear guard formed a line. The dragoons had caught up too quickly. They charged down the riverbank. The rear guard held its ground. The others pushed on through the river.

Shots cracked. Some of the rear guard fell. The horsemen closed in. Finally the guard fired its own musket volley. Three dragoons flew from their horses in heaps. The rear guard broke and ran into the river. Alone Newsome charged, setting himself against the middle of the line of dragoons, one pistol in each hand.

The crack of his pistols sounded feeble. He drew his sword and, raising it high, tilted at the red line. He was surrounded and, in one awful moment, he was cut down. His riderless horse ran into the woods.

The dragoons stampeded into the river after the rear guard.

A cannon's boom, then another, rumbled across the river. Water exploded to one side of the riders, then the other. Dragoons scattered and retreated back up the bank. The rear guard was going to make it. All but the five or six left at the water's edge. And their captain.

Kate turned, back against the boulder, and sagged to the ground. Her throat constricted. Newsome had given his life so the others would have a chance.

Michael slumped next to her. "Those guys got guts. Taking that charge. And Newsome. He had to know he was going down."

Kate had never seen death before. She felt her lower lip quivering. She wanted to say something, the sacrifice, the heroism. But when she tried, her lip jumped uncontrollably. Her voice was stuck. She tried to swallow the lump in her throat, but that only pushed out tears from her eyes. Faces of the marching men flashed in her mind. The questioning expressions. The frightened ones. The stern, hard looks. Which were lying now in the courtyard? Which at the river with their captain? Which wouldn't go home again?

"Hello." A deep voice spoke from behind them.

John stood tall, smiling gently, crookedly.

Michael stood.

Kate began to sob.

"He didn't make it," Michael said in a low voice.

Kate quieted, waiting for John's reaction.

"Pardon?"

"Captain Newsome. He didn't make it. He went down covering his men at the ford."

John gazed toward the ford away in the distance. "He was a good officer." He cleared his throat. "And he

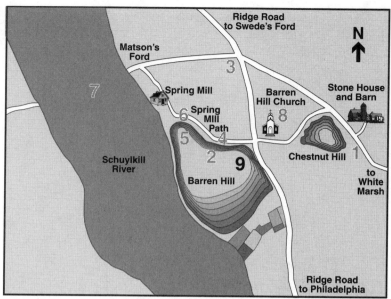

9   Michael and John encounter British dragoons

was a good man. An honorable man. He's passed from us with valor and he has gone to his reward. May the good Lord be waiting with open arms."

When John turned back toward them, the track of a single tear glistened on his cheek. Tears welled in Kate's eyes.

John cleared his voice again. "It's not over yet. Our danger is just beginning. The British will probably go back to Philadelphia. They don't want to be seeing General Washington marching over from Valley Forge. But we've got to be ready in case they scout this hill first."

"We've got a good spot down in the woods. That's where we left Meadow," Michael said.

"I know. I came up through those woods. Left my horse with him. I noticed he's not tethered. Don't you worry he'll wander off?"

"Not a chance."

"Guess you're right. It seemed like he was trying to hide from me. That's quite an animal."

"One of the two best I've ever known," Michael said.

"Still, you two should be more careful. If I wore a red coat, you'd be in chains by now. I guess the General was right, you two did need checkin' on." John leaned against the boulder. "Let's set awhile and talk. We've got some time before I go."

"Where do you have to go?" Michael asked.

"Scouting. Then to report to the General. But I'll have to give the British time to clear out."

John leaned against the boulder, surveying the panorama.

"So, Michael, you say we're related?"

"Yeah. That's what I was told."

"What's the relation?"

"You are . . . I am . . . "

John laughed. His eyes twinkled.

"He means you're from the same line," Kate said.

"The same line?" John asked.

"Yeah, like you and Michael's father are from the same line, the same ancestors. You know the same family."

"I've never heard of you. What's your father's name?"

"Ronald," Michael said.

"Don't believe I've heard of him either. Are your people from around here?"

"Ah, well—west of here a ways."

"You belong to Kate's family?"

"Belong?" Michael asked.

"You their slave?"

"Definitely not. We're free, same as Kate's family."

"Well, so am I. But the same as Kate, I doubt it." John laughed. "Pardon me, miss." John nodded to Kate.

"How did you get to be free?" Kate asked.

"Not the first time white folks have asked me that," John said. "I was born free. My Momma and Daddy were slaves, though. But Daddy had a way with horses. He worked for himself on Sundays and his master let him keep the money he earned."

That word, "master", stung Michael.

"People from all over Goochland County hired my Daddy for all kinds of horse problems. He saved his money and bought his and Momma's freedom."

"He still working with horses?" Michael asked.

"No. He took a chill the winter of '73 and passed on. But he kept up long enough to buy a farm. And now it's mine. My younger brother Jacob is looking after it while I'm gone."

At the mention of "Jacob", Michael and Kate exchanged a glance. Michael's little brother was Jacob, too.

"And beside farmin', I work with horses. Folks say I've got the gift, too. That's why I'm a dragoon."

"What do you mean?" Michael asked.

"Well, when ol' Colonel Theodorik Bland set about puttin' together his company of light dragoons, he recruited only white gentlemen. Those rich enough to buy their own equipment. We've got our farm and all, but we're not rich, that's for certain. And I ain't white, in case you ain't noticed." Banks smiled and his eyes twinkled. "Anyway, I have a good horse, and most of them gentlemen had hired me for horse troubles. So when I joined up with the Continentals, they asked me to join Bland's Horse. Ridin's better than walkin'—that's for sure.

"Then, last December, General Lafayette asked the Colonel to find him a good horse. And the Colonel asked me. So I picked one and took it to the Marquis. Been with him ever since."

"How'd you get to be free, Michael?"

"I've always been free. I figured my people had been slaves, but hearing you talk—I realize I don't really know that."

"How could it be you don't know something like that?"

"No one ever told me. I guess it's been forgotten over the years."

"You can't forget a thing like slavery. You shouldn't."

"That's true." Michael looked down, then back to John.

"You got to ask your elders. You got to find out."

"With them having slavery and all, why did you sign up to fight?" Michael asked.

"I struggled over it. In Goochland County, eight or nine of every ten Africans are slaves—somebody's property—bought and worked and sold. But folks are talking about independence and liberty. And this is my country, too. If I leave it to others to do the fightin', then I don't see as how I can claim my share of it. And equality, well, I'm nudging it along every way I can. And fighting for *my* country is what I can do right now."

He had no idea how hard and long the road toward equality would be. And they certainly couldn't tell him.

Banks looked hard at Michael's space-age riding shoes. His brow furrowed and he looked to Kate, then back to Michael. "I thought you said you were from around here somewhere."

"Just visiting," Michael said.

"Are you two on the run? You have trouble at home?"

"No. What do you mean?" Michael asked.

"Well, you haven't told me where you're from. You say you're free, but don't say how. You're here with a white girl. And from the start something about you don't seem, I don't know, regular. Like those boots. What's it all about?"

Michael looked at Kate.

What could they tell him?

"We overheard the British soldiers and it was our duty to warn the General. That's all," Kate said.

"Where are you really from?"

"Far away, John. The frontier." A frontier of time, though, not country.

"Goochland County ain't that far from the frontier. Where abouts is this frontier?"

Michael was at a loss for what to say. Kate jumped in. "You'd pass a lot of time traveling to get there. It's over the mountains."

"I don't know whether to believe you." Banks looked back from Kate to Michael. "You don't talk clear."

Finally a chance to get to know John and he was suspicious. Couldn't blame him, but it wasn't okay. Got to say the right thing. Something that would bring him in. Got to keep it real.

Michael looked him straight in the eye. "You're right, John. Kate and I have some secrets. We can't exactly talk straight to you about those. But you've got to believe me, the secrets only have to do with how we got here and where we came from. We can't tell anybody that, not even you. But you got to know that we're trying to help, that's the straight truth. We had to save the General. And I wanted to help you, any way I could."

"So we are related? That part's true?"

"Definitely. That's why we rode to the church. 'Cause you're someone close." Michael felt his throat tighten with emotion. His eyes tingled with that light burning that meant tears. He held them in.

"Well, I don't see how getting yourselves killed will help me. But I believe you."

Michael was relieved. He fought with his emotions and waited for his throat to relax. Kate seemed to know.

"Are you married?" she asked.

"Yes, ma'am, to the sweetest woman around—my Sally." John's eyes twinkled. "And we've got a son. Little James."

For a moment, John had a far away look and a sad smile. Then he rejoined them. "They're back on the farm with my brother, Jacob, and my old Mama." John looked at Michael. "I'd like to hear about your branch of the Banks family."

"Well, I've got a brother named Jacob, too. My mother is a teacher, and my father is a pilot." As Michael uttered "pilot", he wished he could take it back. Would John start doubting him again?

"On what river?"

Michael sighed. Even in 1778 there were pilots—on boats.

"He pilots—over the Mississippi," Michael said. Another vague answer, but still technically true—thousands of feet over the Mississippi.

John gazed out over the barren hilltop.

"Redcoats on the move," he said. "See the columns beyond the church. Looks like the General was right. They're retreating to Philadelphia." John looked down to their left. "And seems they've already left the path to the ford. When they clear out of the church, I'll go."

"John?"

"Yes, young lady."

"Do you have anything to eat? We haven't had anything for a long time."

"Sure I do." He pulled a cloth wrap from his knapsack. "I've got some dried rabbit."

He handed Kate and Michael some jerky. Michael tore a bite. Pretty good. Michael smiled as Kate bit off a mouthful. She never would have tried it back home.

"Thank you, John," she said.

He nodded.

"You're good with horses, Michael, the way you handle Meadow. You understand him. And he seems to understand you."

"You shoulda seen the way Michael got us away from the sentry," Kate said. "Meadow reared up, right on cue, and sent him flying."

"I believe it. You know, I never met anybody else who had the gift, like me and my father. But I'm thinking that you do, Michael."

"Riding's just about all I ever want to do. But some people think I shouldn't—just because I'm black. Like riding's only for whites."

"It's the same around here, Michael. About other things. People try to put limits on folks because they have black skin. Don't let them." John shook his head. "If you do, you're still a slave, in a manner of speaking —dancing to someone else's tune. That's what I'm gonna teach little James, if I get home from this war.

"Well, enough small talk. I see the red has cleared out of the church. I'm gonna have a look around."

"I'll come with you," Michael said.

"No, Michael."

"I can handle myself."

"I don't doubt it, but it'd be safer for me if I only have to worry about myself. Then my dear Sally will get to see me again in one piece."

Michael nodded. "I guess you're right." But no way was he going to let John ride away again and leave him stuck waiting on the hilltop.

John headed into the woods.

"Michael, doesn't he remind you of your dad?"

"What do you mean?"

"They look so much alike. His voice sounds just like Mr. B's. And his smile. It's just the same."

"I guess. He is family. But what's getting to me is he's not only my family's past, he's its future."

"I don't get what you mean."

"That story he told, about his parents, and Sally and James and all—that's my own family's past. But if he dies today, my family has no future."

"Yeah."

"I can't just sit here and wait 'til it's too late. After he goes, I'm gonna follow."

"But what if something happens?"

"I'll take my gear. If something happens to me, you can walk back to the stone house and go home."

"I don't like this, Michael."

"If you're not here when I get back, I'll look for you on the way to the house."

"How long should I wait before . . . ?"

"A few hours. That way you'll get half way by dark. You'll make it by noon tomorrow, easy."

John rode over the crest and stopped. "Stay out of sight. Make sure Meadow is ready to go. If you're not here when I get back, I'll look for you at the Spring Mill."

"Be careful, John," Kate said.

"I will," he whispered.

When John turned to ride down the hill, Michael sprang over the crest and into the woods. In a minute he was back, riding Meadow.

"Toss me my gear," he said.

Kate grabbed the knapsack, sorted the gear and handed Michael one set. He stuffed it in the saddlebag.

"Do you really have to go?"

"Got to, Kate. This is my time."

"I really don't want to go back alone. Be careful."

"Definitely." Michael smiled a crooked little smile, turned Meadow and rode away.

eleven

Kate watched John descending the broad, flat hill toward the church with Michael following at a distance.

Of course Michael couldn't sit on this hilltop with his family hanging in the balance. Did he ever wonder why him? Probably not. But why her? Kate was ashamed of the thought. Didn't want to get stuck on that. Should be more like Michael. Anyway, the answer to why her was easy—because she could help a friend who really needed it.

He'd get back. Everything would be okay. But that thought was invaded by images of the still bodies at the ford and church. And the faces—random faces of marching men. Grey and lifeless, except for the eyes. The eyes still pleaded for the news she hadn't brought—turn back, your job is finished. Now it was too late for them. Was it too late for Michael? For John?

John was heading west toward the old church. Last night they had followed him on that same road. It seemed like ages ago.

Something moved in Kate's peripheral vision. Or had it?

Kate scanned the hillside. Nothing. Had she imagined it? The instant she looked back toward John, she saw something out of the corner of her eye. Five or six British dragoons emerged from behind a stand of trees. They headed east on the Spring Mill path. Right toward the church—and John.

They were riding slowly. They hadn't seen John. He hadn't seen them either. But Michael had. Meadow sprinted toward John.

Kate held her breath as John and the dragoons rode unwittingly toward each other.

Michael reached John where Ridge Road met the Spring Mill path. As they stopped together for a moment, the dragoons spotted them and dashed into a gallop.

"Go, Michael, please."

Michael and John sprang away. Clods of dirt flew behind them as their horses dug in. They galloped south on Ridge Road.

Three dragoons kept up the chase, following Michael and John down the road. But the other two broke from the chase and, leaving the road, headed toward the foot of Barren Hill.   •

What were they doing? Then she knew. It was a trap. Soon Michael and John would have a choice—either keep riding south toward the British army—or turn off the road to their right, onto the hillside and into those two dragoons.

"Don't turn, don't turn." Kate crossed her fingers.

But they turned. And the trio followed.

Kate had to do something. She yelled, jumped and waved. But they were too far away to hear her calls, and too busy to notice her antics.

She fell silent. It was too late. Michael and John topped the rise into the ambush. The two dragoons rode between Michael and John like a wedge, but right past them. The way the dragoons jerked their heads as they passed, Kate couldn't tell who was more surprised.

Still at full gallop, Michael swerved back toward the church, and John turned back up the hill, toward Kate.

The dragoons desperately tried to reverse directions. One tried to pull his horse around in a tight circle. The horse refused and charged straight ahead. The rider fought him until he came under control and bounded after John. The other dragoon, trying to stop in his tracks, pulled so hard on the reins the horse turned sideways, stumbled and nearly rolled. But he regained his balance and joined the chase after John.

The three trailing dragoons caught up and all five were after John. They fanned out behind him. He wouldn't be able to turn and they were heading right for Kate. She ducked behind the boulder. She had to get into the woods before they got any closer. She slung the knapsack on her shoulder, scampered over the crest and hid behind the first big tree she could reach.

Michael galloped up the hill behind the dragoons. As John reached the bluff, shots rent the air like thunder that echoed, lingering for just an instant.

John was thrown. His horse's face turned expressive. In a single instant it looked puzzled, then worried, and knowing something was terribly wrong, it tumbled and rolled. Kate screamed inside her brain. She wanted to hide her eyes, but couldn't look away. Then John was up. Thank goodness. And running over the crest toward the woods. But his horse didn't move from the cloud of dust where it had fallen.

John reached the thicket and disappeared fifty yards downhill of her. Two dragoons jumped from their horses and followed him. The three others rode up and down the tree line, their horses prancing and hopping.

Michael and Meadow raced over the crest. Michael jumped down on the run. Another thunder clap from a dragoon's gun and Michael dove into the woods.

Was he hit? Oh, no.

More gunshots shattered the air, so loud it was hard to think.

John burst from the woods with a dragoon crouched in a sprint after him. Then in a seamless motion, John stopped, turned and fired. The charging dragoon straightened up as though he had hit a wall, then crumpled to the ground.

Another dragoon raised his pistol at John's back. But before he could fire, Michael lunged from the woods wielding his own pistols. Running at the dragoon, he fired once. Then again. The dragoon just stood there. Both shots had missed.

Michael was frozen in his tracks under the dragoon's careful aim when Meadow bolted from nowhere. He reared at the dragoon and crashed his hoof like a bludgeon onto the man's head. He crashed into a heap. Meadow snorted, neck arched, nostrils flared and ears pinned back. Kate half expected him to breathe fire.

"Run, Meadow, run," Michael yelled and the horse charged across the hilltop.

The three mounted dragoons converged, swords glistening, and herded Michael and John among them.

Kate couldn't hear them, so she made her way closer, through the thicket down the hill. She hid at the edge of the woods.

A dragoon examined the soldier John shot. "He's dead." Then he knelt by the soldier Meadow had hammered. "He's out, but he ain't topped."

"Let's kill these two." A dragoon menaced Michael and John with his sword.

"Keep your blade clean. They go back so the generals can have at 'em. We'll stay the night at the church and deliver them in the morning."

The soldiers tied their hands behind their backs, then bound John's wrists to Michael's. They pitched the dead soldier over his horse and propped the groggy man in his saddle.

"There's another!" A dragoon pointed at Kate. She had gotten too close. The man ran at her.

Kate turned and fled headlong into the woods. So thick she couldn't see where she was going—she just plunged downhill in great, blind bounds. She was flying until one foot hit wrong and she thudded into the undergrowth. Perfectly still, she lay where she had fallen. Twigs in her face, leaves closing her eyes, she didn't move.

Leaves and branches rustled. Closer. Closer. She dared not look. What if part of her was sticking out? Visible, an ostrich with its head in the sand.

"Come out of there," a voice yelled. "Give it up."

She held her breath. The rustling stopped.

"The forest is likely teeming with them. We best take our leave, while we can."

More rustling. Was it receding? Couldn't tell for sure. Kate released her breath slowly. Yes, the sounds were moving away.

She dared a peek. Couldn't see anything in that thicket. She rolled to a crouch. The leaves made so much noise! But there were no other sounds of rustling. She inched her way back up the hill.

By the time she worked her way back to where she could see, the dragoons were heading down the hill toward the church, driving Michael and John before them.

Kate was the only hope for Michael and John. She had to follow them. But carefully. The dragoons kept looking into the woods.

She moved not a muscle until the group had moved a safe distance downhill. Then she scampered from tree to tree, trying to tread silently across the leafy ground.

Every forest sound made her uneasy. But little by little, she became accustomed to them. They became soothing. A bird's call or a squirrel's chitter made the forest seem as if all were in order. The loamy smell of the soil was comforting.

Then she heard something that didn't belong. Footsteps? She lunged to a large tree and pressed her back against it. But, as she stopped, so did the sound.

Leaves rustled off to her right. She turned quickly. No one. She listened. Nothing but the innocent forest sounds. The tree trunk was hard against her back and it steadied her. Fear was not going to stop her.

She leaned forward. Then, as swift and quiet as an apparition, she scurried, tree to tree, until finally she could see the church beyond the crossroads.

The riders pushed Michael and John through the gate in the stone wall. There were other red-coated soldiers in the churchyard. One of them was African American. Kate couldn't hear them, but she could read their gestures as greetings.

On hands and knees, she inched as close as she dared.

A dragoon led John and Michael through the arched doorway in the steeple. They had just crossed the threshold when the soldier raised his musket and butted John in the back of the head. Kate could almost feel the force of it. As the door closed, John tumbled to the floor, pulling Michael down on top of him.

Kate had to get help. Lafayette. There was no one else. But she could never reach the river before dark. And how could she get across?

Kate sensed a chill that someone was lurking behind her. She turned. Meadow stood in the woods, watching her.

Not alone anymore, her tension eased and she began devising a plan.

"Meadow," she whispered, "I'm going to ride you. Okay?" She led him a short distance up the hill.

"Here goes nothin'." She reached her left foot up into the stirrup. But it was so high she couldn't get any leverage to step up. With her left foot in the stirrup, she began hopping on her right foot. With each hop, she got a bit higher. Meadow stood stone still. One more time, and with a pull on the saddle, she was up. She swung her leg over.

"We did it, Meadow."

He nickered.

The view was different from the driver's seat. Meadow's chestnut mane was thick and glossy. The arch of his neck made him seem so strong and confident. Kate resisted the urge to let Meadow take over. She patted his neck. He nickered again, then snorted.

They worked their way through the edge of the woods at a painstaking crawl. The afternoon light was fading. There was no time to lose. She let Meadow pick their pace while she concentrated on her plan.

How would she get across the river? Ride Meadow down the Spring Mill path and cross at the ford? No. Not the path. Might be British. Not the ford, either. They'd be watching the ford. But she had to cross that river. Either swim it, or ride Meadow. Couldn't ride him down from the bluff. Way too steep. And how could she ride across? She'd never ridden in a river before. It was probably really deep. It was definitely wide. Could Meadow swim that far? It was no good. She'd just have to leave Meadow.

She would climb down that sheer slope and swim the river. And when she reached the other side, she'd just hike to Lafayette's camp.

By the time they reached the bluff, Kate's plan was settled, except for one thing. What about her gear?

She swung her leg over, slid off of Meadow and began to pace. Without the gear, she couldn't get home. Saving Michael but losing the gear would mean living here forever. Why did this have to happen to her? The thought came only once, silenced by the strength of the answer. Because she was the right one. The only one. And she would just do it.

She'd hide the gear behind some tree. Probably nobody would find it. She imagined a red-coated soldier rummaging around the tree trunks. Maybe she'd be able to find it again. She imagined herself going from tree to tree in this great thicket trying to remember which tree hid the gear. Maybe it would stay dry. She imagined a spring shower falling as she searched. Too many maybes.

She could put it into Meadow's saddlebag. That's what Michael had done. Was his still in there? She strode to Meadow and touched the saddlebag. Something was. She reached in and pulled out Michael's gear. Good that the dragoons didn't have it.

Now she would have to decide for both of them where best to leave the gear. Michael probably hadn't expected to be separated from Meadow, so he hadn't actually entrusted Meadow with it. But Kate knew that had he been there, Michael would have wanted to leave it with Meadow. For sure, nobody would catch Meadow unless he wanted to be caught. But would he come back? He had before. She had to rely on Meadow.

She took her gear from the knapsack and stuffed all of it back into the saddlebag.

"Meadow, it's up to you." She patted his neck, turned and headed for the brink.

Meadow whinnied and reared. His hooves pawed the air. Then he pounded them back to the ground. He reared again. A warning.

"Halt!" A red-coated soldier was running toward her.

Kate ran for the brink. It was so steep. The man was still running at her. Kate stepped over the edge, slipped and plopped hard. Feet in the air, she was falling, skidding on her back down the slope.

twelve

Michael and John were tied back to back, so Michael hadn't seen John hit by the musket butt. But the force of the blow had knocked John to the floor with such force that Michael had been yanked off his feet and pulled down on his back on top of John. Michael's position was awkward, vulnerable and uncomfortable. All he could see was the ceiling of the church. Then he saw a man wielding a musket right above his head. The guy was gonna bash him.

"No," someone yelled. Then another man placed himself between Michael and the musket. It was a black man.

"Get out of the way, boy," yelled the musket man.

"Stand easy!" Another man had entered the church. "I told you before we will save these two for the Generals. Now lower your musket."

Musket man did as he was told. Obviously this other guy was the boss.

"Now outside until your head cools a bit," the boss said. After the musket man left, the boss said, "Thank you for stemming that bit of mischief."

"You're welcome, sir," the black man said.

"These two killed one of our dragoons. Vengeance is to be expected. But if they're dead, they can't very well answer questions. I'd like you to stand watch over them for a while."

"Yes, sir."

"And see if you can rouse that one."

"I'll do my best, sir."

Michael was still splayed above John's immobile body, pinioned by his wrists to John. As the boss left the church, Michael began to worry about John. He hadn't moved since they collapsed.

"My name's Samuel. I'm gonna try to get you up."

"Thanks," Michael said. "Is he all right?"

"Well, he's breathing. I can't untie you, but I'm gonna need your help," Samuel said.

"Whatever I can do," Michael said.

"I'll get him sitting. Then he can lean on you."

"I'm ready."

Samuel grabbed John around the chest, pulling and

rolling him, until he and Michael were sitting, back to back.

"Now, over here," Samuel said. They scooted John toward a bench and let him slump against it.

Samuel slapped John lightly on the face several times. John groaned, rolled his head and then dropped off again.

Samuel pulled a chair over and sat a few feet way. "I'd say he'll come out of it. But it'll take a while." He leaned over and pulled off Michael's cap. "You're just a boy."

"I'm old enough," Michael said.

"Old enough to get yourself in some trouble. Old enough to see the West Indies." Samuel shook his head. "I heard it's even worse than here."

"Maybe you can help us get away?"

"Then I'd end up in the Indies. I ain't goin' back to slave for the likes of you."

"Don't you want to help a brother?"

Samuel's laugh was mocking. "You, bro, chose to stand beside the men who call themselves masters. I ran from slavery to stand against those men. Now I'm free, I plan to stay free."

"Why'd you stop that guy from clubbing me?"

"'Cause I've seen too much of that in my life. But I got no special sympathy for you. You made your choice, now you got to live with it."

The boss walked back into the church. "Able to rouse him?"

"No, sir. But he moved his head."

"Well, that's something. He's got to be able to travel by morning. Now, what about this one?"

"He's fine. Just a child, though."

"So, they're resorting to children, now," the boss said. "What errand were you on, son?"

"Errand?" Michael asked.

"Come now, son. It won't help you to play the fool. Why didn't you run with your General Lafayette?"

"I'm not a Continental. I'm with the militia."

"Which militia?"

"The Virginia Militia."

"And what were you doing on Barren Hill today?"

"Trying to deliver a message to General Lafayette."

"Yes?"

"That the Virginia Militia had arrived at White Marsh." Michael didn't feel right about talking so freely, but Lafayette had told him to say all this.

"That was the entire message?"

"Yes."

"Any documents?"

"No."

"We may find out different if we catch that horse of yours."

"No, you won't. There aren't any documents."

"How many men with the militia?"

"I don't know."

"Surely you expected Lafayette to ask such a question. What would you have answered?"

"Same thing I'm telling you. I don't know."

The boss turned to Samuel. "Hand me your knife."

"Yes, sir."

The boss took the knife from Samuel and held it with the point pressing against the side of Michael's neck. "Breathe easy. I'm not going to damage you. I'll leave that to the Generals." He pressed the point a little harder. "But remember, it won't help you to play the fool.

"Move across the room," the boss said to Samuel. "And don't talk with him. I want him to think about how he'll answer tomorrow." The boss handed the knife to Samuel and left the building.

After Samuel moved, John moaned softly.

"John? Are you okay?"

He moaned again.

thirteen

Kate couldn't stop her fall. She dug in with her heels and clawed at the gravelly dirt with her hands. But it was too loose. Jagged rocks pummeled and raked her as she skidded, faster and faster.

She had one last chance before becoming airborne and tumbling all the way to the bottom. A scrawny bush clung to the hillside below her. She had to get it. She slid toward it, then passed it. With a last gasp, she rolled and clenched a slim branch with her right hand. It stopped her, but she could feel it giving way. She stabbed with her left and clasped another branch as the

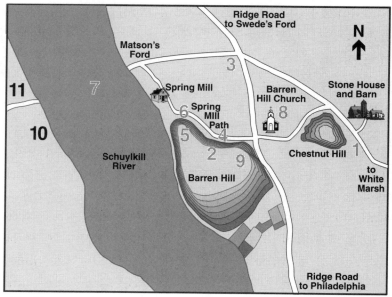

10   Kate meets Collins
11   Lafayette's new camp

first broke. It held long enough for her to grasp the small trunk. Holding tight with both hands, she hung there afraid that any movement would be too much for the scrawny bush.

She looked up. Fifty feet above, the soldier was carefully making his way down. Slow, but he was coming.

Her left elbow twinged. Her tail bone ached. She didn't even want to look at her stinging hands and forearms. If not for the knapsack shielding her back, it would have been even worse.

Kate gathered her wits and pulled her feet beneath her. This time she'd be ready. She raised to a sitting crouch and, releasing the bush, began a slower, controlled slide on her feet. Almost like snowboarding. A few times she slipped to one side, aggravating her sore hands, but she never really lost control. She was getting pretty good at it. Finally, the slope leveled at the bottom of the hill and she came to a stop near the river's edge.

She looked back up the hill. The soldier was still making his way, but her slide had left him far behind. Then she saw Meadow silhouetted against the sky. Though he was far above her, he seemed enormous. Kate imagined wings sprouting from his back, like some mythical horse. He whinnied again, as if in farewell, then turned and disappeared behind the ridge.

Daylight was all but gone. The opposite riverbank looked far off. Seemed like a mile. With the currents, it would probably take her an hour. Her stomach ached for food. An hour was a tough swim anytime. Hungry, she might not make it. This would be the swim of her life.

She looked back up the hill. The soldier was getting closer.

A chill tightened her spine. It would be pitch dark before she finished. She imagined unknown creatures swimming below in the dark water. And she felt the familiar jitters coming on. She hated that feeling. But today there was no question. She would do this. She breathed deeply as she undressed. Each exhale calmed her.

Kate stripped down to her underwear. She stuffed the clothing and boots in the knapsack, leaving behind only the militia shirt and cap. She put it around her waist, pulled it tight and buckled it. Once it was water-logged the pack would be heavy. But snug against her lower back, she hoped, it wouldn't hamper her too much.

She prepared herself for the river to be icy, like a mountain lake, bone numbing. The cold would be like a big fist squeezing her chest, making it harder and harder to breathe. No matter how cold, she would just keep swimming. There was no other way.

She looked back one last time. The soldier had stopped. He was trying to settle his footing to shoot at her.

Kate padded into the river and dove under. She stayed under as long as she could, swimming through the green mucky water. It wasn't icy at all. Just cool.

When she surfaced, she saw the soldier trying to pick his way back up the slope. And in the dusky light, she could see a large rock outcropping on the far side of the river. That would be her goal and her guide against being swept off course by the current. She'd have to fight it because Lafayette's camp was upstream and the current would push her away from her goal. Near the shore it wasn't too strong. How would it be out in the middle?

Kate leaned forward and glided into the water. The coolness soothed her stinging hands and arms. She put her face into the water and began her strokes, taking a breath after every third stroke, first on her left side then on her right. She counted silently, almost like a chant, one, two, three, breathe, one, two, three, breathe. The rhythm calmed her.

Images played in her mind's eye. The church door opens. Michael and John stumble through the door. The musket comes down across the back of John's head. He collapses. Michael is pulled down, no hands free to break his fall. The door closes with an exaggerated clank, like a prison door in the movies.

Kate's rhythm was broken by the image of Meadow on the hilltop, his face set, his nostrils flared. She stopped stroking. Treading water, she looked across the river to get her bearings. Nearly halfway. She strained to see her rock in the gathering darkness. Was that it? Only a little upstream. The current hadn't carried her off too far.

She would just aim a little upstream of her target. That meant swimming more against the current. It would be harder, but she could do it.

Plunking her face into the water, she set out with the current pushing against her right shoulder. Her strokes felt strong. The water seemed like syrup, so thick she could almost grab it and pull herself through it. One, two, three, breathe, one, two, three, breathe.

Time was suspended. No distractions. Nothing to hear. Nothing to see in the dark water. Only her rhythm and her thoughts.

She hoped the wrist gear was safe. What would she do, living the rest of her life in the eighteenth century? And if she didn't get help, she would be left alone.

Michael and John would be sold into slavery. She pulled harder. "One, two, three, breathe."

Meadow's silhouette flashed in her mind so she stopped to check her progress. The sky was nearly as dark as the water, but she could make out the tree line behind the river. Couldn't see the rock, though. Couldn't tell how far downstream she'd been swept. Gliding her face into the water, she set out again, guided only by the current.

With the relentless flow pushing against her right shoulder, Kate began to tire. She was hungry, a little light headed, and fatigue stabbed her shoulders. Her stroke began to break down. She knew the feeling well, the waning strength, the shortened reach, the imbalanced pull. Her arms grew heavier and weaker. The water seemed so thin her strokes were pinwheels in a breeze, spinning but going nowhere. Each stroke brought the knifing pain. She told herself she could still go a long way, but doubt intruded. She struggled to get back into her rhythm and push the fatigue from her mind.

She imagined her room at home, her cozy bed, her dresser covered with favorite things. She tried to picture the school cafeteria, the lunch line, kids sitting at tables. Walking down the hall at school, kids talked and laughed, going in every direction. Jamal and James sauntered. And always in the background, one, two, three, breathe. She thought of riding with Michael to the Lucky Star. Riding Midnight up the

steep trail behind the barn. They crested the trail—
Meadow reared.

Kate stopped and lifted her face. She tried to see
where she was. But everything was black. Eyes open
or closed—no different. She couldn't even see which
way to go. Her enemy, the current, had become her
only guide. She kept it at her right shoulder and glided
back into her stroke. One, two, three, breathe.

The ache became undeniable. Thoughts of home no
longer could distract her. She was afraid to stop. Afraid
to look again into that featureless blackness. Fighting
panic. Just follow the current.

Her hand hit something. Mud! She grabbed a squishy
fistful and pumped it high in the air.

She floated there for just a moment resting in the
shallows and savoring the end of the swim. When she
stood, the river muck oozed between her toes. She felt
the impulse to run, but couldn't. The bottom was scattered with slimy, slippery rocks and the night was just
too dark. So she treaded with care, wincing at every
sludgy step until she wobbled up the riverbank and
collapsed, cross-legged on the dirt.

She unbuckled the knapsack from around her waist.
In it, her clothes were soaked, shirts dripping and jeans
soggy. She wrung them out the best she could and
wrestled to put on her tee shirt. The old blouse slipped
on easier, but the jeans clung. She had to work them
over her feet inch by frustrating inch. Trying to hurry
only made it worse. And so did the darkness. Finally

the hems cleared her heels and she stood to work the waistband the rest of the way up.

Her boots were just as bad. The sodden laces just wouldn't give. She had to loosen them by feel all the way down.

Chilled by the night air in her wet clothes, she began to shiver. Shivers turned to quakes as she struggled to slide her boots on and tighten the laces.

Time to get moving. Maybe that would warm her up. She would stay along the riverbank. The sound would be her guide upstream to the camp. She'd have to feel her way along in the dark. With the sting of her slide down Barren Hill still fresh, she probed for safe footing with pointed toe. With every step her boots gurgled and squished. So much for stealth.

The riverbank was smooth and she was making surprisingly good progress. Feeling pretty lucky and taking it for granted, she stopped bothering to probe. As she walked, she strained to see the firelights of camp.

Then, she heard a chilling sound. Rustling, rumbling that somehow Kate knew was the sound of something big. Something heavy. Something dangerous. And the sounds were rumbling closer. Instinct took over and in the dark she ran. But midstep her foot snagged, tipping her off balance and sending her down, face first. She threw her hands up to protect her face, and crunched into a thorny clump of bushes. Fighting panic, she rasped herself free from countless little spikes. Fiery new scratches crisscrossed the old and there she stood, night-blind, panting and listening. The rumble started again, bearing down even faster.

Only one clear path in the darkness. She turned and ran back to the river's edge and splashed into the water. The bottom wasn't as squishy here, but it was more crowded with slippery rocks and her boots slipped with every step. But with every step she got deeper until she could float. She strained to hear, but the rumbling had stopped.

No way was she going back to shore. It was too slow anyway. In the river, she could float and push off the bottom in a kind of swim-walk. This was much faster than inching through the brambles and much better than worrying about that rumbling. Soon Kate saw the firelight of camp.

As she closed in on the camp, she could see there were campfires right along the shore. She hit a stretch of shallows, where she lifted her feet high and sloshed along. Her steps were noisy and the soldiers heard her. Kate could hear them talking.

"Someone or something is out there."

"I hear it."

"Help, help!" Kate yelled.

"Who goes there?"

"My name is Kate. I need to see General Lafayette. It's an emergency." Kate continued slogging toward them.

"Is that Kate, our own militiaman?"

"Collins?"

"Yes, ma'am."

"Thank goodness. I've got to talk to the General. They've got Michael and John."

"Let's go."

Collins led her to a path as the moon, a big, orange globe, was rising above the tree line. Before long, they entered a camp much like the one on Barren Hill and went directly to the lone grouping of tents. Major Gimat sat at a small table with a lantern. As they jogged up, he stood.

"What is this?"

"Please, I need to speak to General Lafayette."

"Get the General!" Gimat barked.

"I am here." Lafayette stepped from a tent and walked toward them. "What has happened, Kate?"

"Private Banks was scouting. There were dragoons. Michael tried to warn him—there was a fight and they took Michael and Private Banks."

"Are they hurt?"

"Yes—well, John is. They hit him in the head."

"Where are they?"

"In the church. They said they'd stay 'til morning. Then they would deliver Michael and John to the Generals."

"How many British?"

"Four dragoons and three others."

"Collins, fetch Captain McLane. And bring a blanket for Kate."

"Yes, sir." Collins ran off.

Lafayette tilted his head and looked at Kate's wet clothing. "And how did you get here, Kate?"

"I swam the river from Barren Hill."

He shook his head slowly. "The river is so wide and treacherous. You are an amazing young woman."

Captain McLane strode up with Collins in his wake and stopped smartly before the General. "Sir."

Collins continued behind Kate. "I've got something of yours," he whispered and draped a shawl over her shoulders. It was her powder blue skirt.

"Captain, I want you to lead a mission of rescue. Two of today's heroes are prisoners. Private Banks and the young man who warned us."

"My pleasure, General."

"They're held at the church by seven British. Take 50 Light Dragoons. Set pickets. Surprise them. Use your discretion, but bring Michael and Banks out safely. Hold the church. We will follow in the morning."

"May I go, too?" Kate blurted.

Lafayette's left eyebrow arched. "Yes, you have earned it. But stay with the pickets." He turned to McLane. "Arrange an escort for the young lady."

"Thank you, General—for everything," Kate said.

"I am honored to be of service, mademoiselle." Lafayette bowed.

A dashing young soldier approached Kate leading two horses.

"Good evening, miss." He took off his hat and bowed deeply.

He was cute. About high school age. She tried to curtsey, but not really knowing how, kind of messed it up. How embarrassing. She pushed her hair back.

"I'm Private Taylor, miss, and I'm to be your escort to the church."

"Hi. I'm Kate."

"Yes, I know, miss."

Miss? Never could get used to that.

"How well do you ride, miss?"

"I can keep up." That sounded more confident than she really was. "You can call me Kate."

"Yes, miss."

Private Taylor webbed his hands like a stirrup. Kate stepped into the web and he gave her a boost into the saddle. As Private Taylor led her horse, Kate shivered in her sopping clothes. Her soggy jeans chafed. She pulled the skirt around her like a cape and tied the waist string around her neck.

Private Taylor led her to a field where horsemen were formed into a column, four abreast. Kate and Private Taylor went to the back of the line.

No sooner had the column started than Kate began to fall behind. Private Taylor held back with her.

The dust from the column billowed and its thunder rolled. The moon was higher and Kate could see the first riders surge into the ford.

"Private Taylor?"

"Please call me Joseph, miss—I mean Kate."

"I've never ridden in a river before, Joseph."

"Just keep the reins loose and the horse will follow the rest. And I'll stay with you."

That last part sounded pretty good.

Their horses splashed into the river together. This was all right. Riding in the moonlight with a personal escort seemed to narrow the river. Her harrowing swim seemed distant.

Up the far bank and onto the open road, they fell further behind.

"There's no rush," Joseph said. "We'll be staying with the pickets at the foot of Barren Hill. We'll just give them a little time to set up before we arrive."

But in only a few minutes, they caught up. The column had stopped on the road between two buildings.

"What's up, Joseph?"

"Pardon, miss?"

"Why'd we stop?"

"They're checking the mill—for irregulars and marauders."

The building on the river side was on a slope, so that the front was one story, but the back had an additional level below. The lower part was stone, the upper was heavy wood planks. The building across the road was smaller and finer, made of loaf shaped stones, mortared in white with white shuttered windows.

"So this is Spring Mill. It looks different."

"Has it changed?" Joseph asked.

"No. I just never saw it up close before."

"But don't you live near here?"

Before Kate could answer, everyone was back on horseback and sprinting away from the mill. The column opened an ever-widening lead over Kate and

Joseph until only the last riders were visible. Soon even they and their cloud of dust vanished.

Having them out of sight made Kate feel somehow less hurried. And with their thunder quieted, she felt the ride turn peaceful. But when they rounded the next bend in the road, all of Kate's feelings were overwhelmed by what she saw.

The bluff towered above the landscape. The full moon, which was above and behind the bluff, cast it in a magical light. From above, the bluff had been so familiar. But from down on the road, it transcended natural heights.

Kate stared spellbound as the silhouette of a horse appeared on that craggy peak. It reared and pawed the air, then treetops blocked her view and the vision was gone. But its valorous impression lingered and Kate's spirits soared like a hawk.

When Kate and Joseph caught up with the others, Captain McLane was conferring with several officers. The Continentals were in the woods, having divided into three groups. With two swings of Captain McLane's arms, the groups began to move this way and that around the church.

Joseph led Kate to a spot in the thicket where, kneeling in the soft humus, she could see everything—the church, the yard and its surrounding stone wall.

The arched double doors in the steeple were opened wide. A British soldier sat at the threshold, legs outstretched and arms folded over his chest. Probably asleep.

A single guard leaned against the stone wall next to the gate.

Kate had seen hostage situations in the movies. "We have you surrounded, come out with your hands up," the police would say. The hostage takers would demand an airplane to some faraway place. Not this time. No negotiators. No demands. But please, no casualties.

"Can they do this?" Kate whispered in Joseph's ear.

"Good chance. There's a back door. Our gents'll burst through front and back. Catch 'em unaware."

A lone Continental slipped over the churchyard wall and crept behind the guard. One flash of his tomahawk and the unsuspecting guard crumpled to the ground. The soldier in the doorway hadn't moved a muscle. Definitely sound asleep.

Continentals poured over the wall and stole to the side of the church.

In the woods, an owl hooted. Another answered, then a third, and the Continentals burst through the double doors shouting and knocking down the sleeping redcoat. A few moments of shuffling inside, some yelling and then all was quiet.

A Continental appeared in the doorway. "All's clear," he yelled waving his arms above his head.

Kate jumped up and ran across the road. Joseph scampered to catch her. By the time she reached the yard, Michael and John were coming out the front doors. She ran right at Michael and gave him a big hug. "Thank goodness," she said.

"Kate, you saved us. I knew you would. I kept telling John."

"Yes, miss. He said you're the best swimmer around and you would bring help. I had my doubts there for a while. But foolish doubts they turned out to be."

"How's your poor head, John?" Kate asked.

"Been better," he said with a crooked grin. "But pretty good right now."

"Miss—ah—Kate, I need to report to the Captain."

"Oh. Well thanks for everything, Joseph." She held out her hand.

"It's been my pleasure, Kate." He took her hand in both of his for a lingering moment, then bowed, turned and walked toward the steeple.

John rubbed his eyes and gingerly touched his wound. "I'm gonna go rest this achin' head. Thank you again, Kate." John bowed, then walked away.

"Good night, John. And feel better," Kate called after him.

"We did it," Kate said. "Lafayette escaped the trap and John's gonna see tomorrow morning."

"Yeah, but it looked bad for a while. Tell me what happened."

"Okay, but let's sit here by the fire. I need to get dry. Here's the short version. I saw you guys get caught and I followed you to the church. I saw that guy hit John, too. Anyway, I rode Meadow back to the bluff."

"So you found Meadow?"

"Yeah. Actually, he found me, but I left him at the bluff. I slid down the cliff and swam the river."

"Just like that, you swam the river?"

Kate smiled. "Yeah."

"Didn't you get nervous?"

"I handled it. And I don't think any little race will ever make me nervous again. Anyway, I found Collins on the other side and he took me to camp."

"And you didn't see Meadow after that?"

"No. Well, actually maybe. I did see a horse on the bluff when we were on the Spring Mill path. But I don't really know if it was Meadow."

"I've got a little problem, Kate. I left my gear in Meadow's saddlebag."

"I know. I found it."

"You have it?"

"No. I left mine there, too," Kate said.

"We've got to have the gear before noon tomorrow."

"But how?"

"What about that horse you saw?"

"We were riding on the Spring Mill path below the bluff. I saw a horse up on the bluff for a second. It was up on its back legs. Then my view got blocked. That's it."

"But you thought it was Meadow?"

"I wanted it to be."

fourteen

Michael hadn't been able to sleep all night. He tossed and turned worrying about the gear. He had to find Meadow. And it had to be early enough that they could still make it back to the wormhole by noon.

As soon as there was a hint of predawn light, he got up and started walking up Barren Hill toward the bluff. It would be a long walk. But it was still really early. No one else was even awake yet.

That horse Kate saw up on the bluff had to be Meadow. There hadn't been any horses just wandering loose. What other horse could it be? A chill came with the answer. Captain Newsome's horse had run into the woods. Could it have made its way up to the bluff?

Michael walked faster. The hill was so big, the bluff so distant. He seemed not to make any progress. He broke into a jog.

The Captain's horse might have gone back to where the original camp had been. That made sense. He could have been on the edge of the bluff in a panic after the battle. That made sense, too. But where else would Meadow go? Kate left him at the bluff. Michael had left him there, too, just before they were captured. The horse Kate had seen on the bluff must have been Meadow. But that was last night. He might be gone by now. Maybe this was just a waste of time. Michael ran harder.

What if Meadow showed up at the church? What would he do if Michael weren't there? Would he run? How much did he really understand?

Michael's mind spun. Needing to catch his breath, he slowed to a walk. His hands coiled and uncoiled. He couldn't stand the slow pace and started to run.

The eastern sky was bright now with the dawn. But Michael headed toward the western horizon, still a dusky blue.

Michael owed Kate. She had come through the wormhole to help. And Mack had been right. Without Kate, he wouldn't have saved John. He couldn't even have saved himself. The whole thing would have failed. And Kate had had to face her fears to do it. She had abandoned her own gear, gambling her own way

home against a chance to rescue them. He couldn't let
her down. The thought of it kept him running, even as
the slope steepened.

After what seemed an eternity, Michael saw a shape
on the hillside. That would be John's horse. As the sky
grew lighter and he got closer, he could clearly see the
still shape of the once graceful animal. All its fluid
power gone to stiffness. He forced himself not to look.

Once beyond the horse, he turned north for the last
part of his journey. He had hoped by now to see
Meadow prancing on the hilltop. He searched along
the tree line into which he and John had run from the
dragoons. Nothing.

Michael's heart began to sink. If Meadow wasn't
here, Michael would never find him in time. He had
gambled everything on his guess that that horse on the
bluff had been Meadow. How could he have been so
stupid? Had he stayed at camp, he could have borrowed a horse and enlisted others to join the search.
They could have covered all directions at the same
time. Instead, he hadn't been able to wait. His impa-
tience was going to be their end.

Now he could clearly see the bluff with its boulder.
No Meadow.

When he finally reached the peak, he was deflated.
He climbed on the big rock and sat down, gazing over
the panorama and hoping to see a horse romping on
the hillside.

The last time he had seen Meadow, he had told him
to run from the dragoons. Meadow had bolted across

that very hillside, as if he understood perfectly. But where was he now? Even when Michael had run to the clearing, fetching Meadow to follow John, Meadow had seemed to understand. He had blasted from the clearing and through the thicket without hesitation. But where was he now? Even John had sensed that Meadow understood he was to stay, untethered, at the clearing. As though he understood the clearing was their hideout.

The clearing. Michael's heart raced. He leaped from the boulder and ran over the crest. This time it was he who blasted through the bramble without hesitation. He had no view of the clearing through the thicket. Leaves and branches gave way before him. His face finally brushed the last leaves and he burst into that sudden open. There was Meadow grazing, his long neck stretched toward the ground. He snapped his head to his full height, his ears peaked and his brow wrinkled. Then the big horse nickered and shook his head up and down.

"I know, I know, it's about time. I was just a little slow to figure it out." Michael took Meadow's face in his hands and put his forehead to Meadow's muzzle. Then he checked the saddlebag.

"Let's go, boy, we've got things to do."

In moments, Meadow was blasting through the woods, one more time, with Michael hunched over his mane. The bramble gave way as if before a gale.

fifteen

Kate awoke to the sounds of soldiers rekindling fires, preparing food and going this way and that. It all seemed remote. She was consumed by thoughts of Meadow and their gear.

"Good morning, Kate."

"Morning, John. How are you feeling?"

"Oh, I'll be fine. Where's Michael?"

"Don't know. Probably looking for Meadow."

"That Meadow is one fine horse. And smart." John stretched the word. "The way he took after that dragoon, he's got fire in him." John's eyes saddened. "It broke my heart to leave my horse on the field that way. Had no choice. Hope he didn't suffer."

Kate remembered the horse's expressions of puzzlement and worry. She couldn't tell John about that. She didn't know what to say. Silence seemed the most respectful. After a while, she asked, "What will you do now, John?"

"Whatever they order me to do. Maybe the General will want me to stay. But without a horse, I don't know. Either way, I'm in it 'til it's over or 'til they carry me off the field."

If only Michael could find Meadow. If they could find their gear, Kate would have her clean, warm, safe world where her biggest worry was feeling nervous at a swim meet. How pointless was that. And ridiculous. Meanwhile, John would probably be without decent food, clothing and shelter. Hungry and cold, he would face the tension of life and death struggles.

Where was Michael? Kate was up pacing and looking.

"Michael will be all right. You don't have to worry," John said.

"You don't understand, John. We've got to find Meadow."

"I understand you want to find the horse. I don't understand why you're so bothered. More of your secrets?"

"Kind of. We've got to get home this morning and we can't without Meadow," Kate said.

"May I offer any assistance?" Captain McLane asked.

"Yes. We need to find Michael," Kate said.

"Again?" Captain McLane laughed. "We just rescued him. He's lost again?"

"We think he went to look for his horse, loose since we were taken near the hilltop yesterday," John said. "Can I borrow a horse, Captain?"

"Take the one Kate rode last night. And maybe a few other riders would help?"

"Yes, sir."

"Find young Taylor. He'll set you up."

"Wait! Is that Michael?" Kate pointed to a horse and rider that had emerged from behind a stand of trees at the hill's edge.

"Might be," John said.

"If not, find Taylor. I'll alert him," Captain McLane said.

"Thank you, Captain."

"You've earned it, Private Banks. I'd be pleased to have you ride with me from now on. If it suits you, I'll ask the General."

"It suits me fine, Captain. But I left my horse on the field yesterday."

"That does pose a problem. We're short of animals. Well, we'll see. In any event, your service has been noted." Captain McLane saluted John and marched off.

The horse and rider were closer now. There was no mistaking Meadow, with his powerful neck arched, loping down the hill.

At the road, they slowed to a walk and came through the gate right up to Kate and John.

Michael's expression revealed nothing about whether he had the gear.

"Well?" Kate rubbed Meadow's neck. She couldn't speak plainly with John standing there. "Is everything *okay?*"

Michael's broad, crooked grin answered her. He swung his leg over and hopped out of the saddle. Patting the saddlebag, he said, "Everything's just fine."

"I'm glad you found him, Michael. That horse is something special," John said.

"Yes, John, he is." Michael stroked Meadow's neck. "Kate and I have to go."

"To the frontier?" John cocked his head.

"Yes, sort of. Can you borrow a horse and ride with us?"

"Yes. I'll be right back."

Kate waited until John had gone. "So you've got the gear?"

"Definitely. Meadow was waiting in the clearing. It just took me a while to figure it out."

John rode up on Kate's horse.

"Let's go," Michael said. He hopped on Meadow and pulled Kate up behind him.

They rode out of the church yard, waving and thanking the soldiers they passed. They headed down the road toward the wagon trail and the stone house.

"Now John," Michael said, "you were saying about how great a horse Meadow is."

"Yes. Special."

"He feels the same about you."

Meadow snorted and stepped a little higher.

"How's that?"

"Well you see, Meadow and I did a lot of talking on the way down the hill."

"You did?" John smiled.

"Definitely. And we've come to a conclusion."

"Pray tell."

"Kate and I can't take Meadow with us—even though I'd love to. *Time* just won't allow it. Anyway, you don't have a horse, and Meadow won't have a rider. So we thought that you two should team up."

"Team up?"

"Yeah, we want you to have Meadow—and we want him to have you."

Meadow nickered and peaked his ears.

"I'm honored. I'll take the best care of him."

"I know you will." Michael's voice caught with emotion.

They turned onto the old wagon trail and headed into the darkness of the forest. Kate eyed it suspiciously, but being up on Meadow made it seem less imposing than it had when they first faced it on foot.

"I've got to ask you for one more thing, John."

"Anything, Michael."

"You've got to trust us one more time, even though it doesn't make sense. A little ways ahead, the woods clear and the trail opens onto a meadow. That's where you've got to leave us."

"On the edge of a meadow?" John asked.

"Yes. I can't explain. Just trust that it'll be all right."

In a few minutes, the clearing was visible ahead as a light at the end of a tunnel. When they cleared the woods, they stopped. Kate slid down and Michael followed.

Michael placed his forehead flat between Meadow's eyes. A final caress, then he backed off. "You take care of ol' John for me, okay?"

Meadow nickered and pawed the ground.

Michael walked to John. Their eyes met and they gripped each other's forearms.

"It's meant a lot to me to meet you, John. It's changed my life. You taught me who I am and where I fit. You make me proud to be who I am." Michael choked out the last words.

"I'm the one who has reason to be proud, Michael. I'm proud to have served with you. Proud that you're family. And I'd be proud if my son grows up just like you." John wrapped Michael in a great, great grandfatherly hug.

"And Kate, I've never known a girl with your courage. I will long tell the story of the young woman who swam a river, swift and wide, to save my life."

Kate ran to hug John. Her eyes streamed with sadness, but a rich sadness it was.

"John, say goodbye and thanks to the General," Michael said.

"Collins and Joseph, too," Kate said.

"I will. But must I leave you here?"

"We have to go on alone, John," Michael said.

"I guess you know best."

Michael pulled the gear from Meadow's saddlebag and patted the big horse one last time.

"Got to go," Michael said.

"You two be careful," John said.

"Same to you, John—for Sally, James and all the future Banks," Michael said.

Kate and Michael turned and walked away.

"Including me," Michael said under his breath.

sixteen

Michael and Kate stopped only once to look back. John and Meadow hadn't moved. Michael and Kate waved, then turned away, toward the old farmhouse and the portal back to their own time. And for the first time since they were little, Michael and Kate held hands walking home.

"Well, there it is," Kate said when the little house came into view.

But the closer they got, the slower they walked. When they finally reached the path leading to the house, they paused, reluctant to leave now that it was finally time to go.

"We better check the time." Michael put on the headgear. "Whoa. Six minutes left. Later than I thought."

They walked the path to the little storage room and put on the wrist gear.

"You know, Michael, I feel a little like I don't want to push this red button."

"After all that, you don't want to leave?"

"No. It's gotten pretty comfortable here. But it's more because I'm afraid it won't work."

"Well now we'll find out." Michael motioned toward the storage room.

"Wait, Michael, I forgot my shoes." Kate ran toward the barn.

"Hurry up, Kate, only five minutes."

Kate ran through the big, double doors and down the wide central corridor to the ladder. Her cross-trainers were in the corner, right where she had tossed them that first day. She sat on a ladder rung to unlace her old boots. She tossed one into the corner, then the other.

"Three minutes," Michael yelled from outside.

"I'm hurrying." Kate slipped on one cross-trainer and was holding the other when she heard a rustling of hay from the loft. She leaned back against the ladder and looked up. A man appeared over the edge of the loft, looking back down at her. For an instant, Kate was spellbound. Then she snapped to. The man was wearing a red coat.

Kate jumped up and ran from the barn, wearing one shoe and carrying the other.

"You there, stop!" The man jumped down the ladder and ran after her.

Michael turned when Kate flew out of the barn door. The red-coated soldier, with bayonet fixed on the end of his musket, ran at them.

"Press it!" Kate yelled.

Michael swung open the old closet door. He pushed his red button and the mouth of the wormhole opened. Kate caught up. Without breaking stride she dropped her shoe, pressed her button and jumped into the rippling light. Michael was right behind her.

The point of the bayonet entered the mouth of the wormhole and dissolved into wavy distortion. Michael followed Kate through the waves into the computer generated hallway. The portal door closed by itself.

Kate exhaled deeply and bent over, resting her hands on her knees.

Michael reached back for the doorknob. "It's locked. I guess it's really over."

They directed themselves past all the doors and, at the end of the hallway, removed the headgear. They were back in Michael's room.

Kate slumped into a chair. "Un—be—lievable."

"Check the time." Michael pointed to the date and time on his computer. "We've been gone just a few minutes."

"A couple of days in 1778 only took a few minutes?"

"Just one of the things Mack was right about. Thanks, Kate."

Kate blushed.

"Michael." His mother called from downstairs.

"Welcome home," Kate whispered.

Michael smiled. His eyes twinkled. "Hi, Mom. Hey, Mom, is it okay if Kate stays for dinner?"

Kate nodded enthusiastically.

"Sure. That'd be nice. Kate, honey, check with your folks."

"Okay, Mrs. B."

"How was Jonathan Apples today?" Mr. B asked when they were all seated for dinner.

His voice sounded so much like John's.

"He's great. Hey, Dad, I've been doing some research." Michael glanced at Kate with a smile. "Did you know one of our ancestors fought in the Revolutionary War?"

"No, I didn't. Nobody talks much about blacks in the Revolution, except about that one guy, Crispus Attucks or something, who died at the Boston Massacre."

"There were a lot of African Americans fighting on both sides and one of them was a cavalryman named John Banks. I bet he was our ancestor."

"No kidding. John Banks."

"Did our family come from Virginia?"

"Yes, way back the Banks lived in Virginia."

"John Banks was from Virginia, too."

"Really."

"Yes. And he had a brother named Jacob."

Michael's little brother looked up.

"Well, Jacob is a family name. That's how we named our Jacob." Mr. B smiled and nodded toward his younger son.

"You seem to know quite a bit about this John Banks," Mrs. B said.

"Yeah, it's like I actually know him." Michael glanced at Kate. "He had an amazing horse named Meadow."

"You know his horse's name?" Mr. B crinkled his forehead.

"Yeah."

"He was famous?" Mr. B asked.

"Meadow was a horse hero," Michael said. "And John had a gift for handling horses."

"Do tell," Mr. B said.

"And I love horses, too."

"Well, that's not exactly news." Mrs. B smiled.

"That's true, but here's some," Michael said. "I'm dedicating my competitive riding to the memory of our ancestor, John Banks, and his awesome horse, Meadow. And I intend to win the championship."

"That's great, Michael. I'm sure John Banks will be watching from up there somewhere," Mr. B said.

After dinner, Michael and Kate cleared the table while Mr. and Mrs. B lingered, talking about their day.

Michael put dishes on the kitchen counter and was standing over the sink.

"Michael, do you think anyone noticed that I came to dinner without shoes?"

"No one would care. I do it all the time," Michael said as he looked out the window. Then it struck him. Rudy's truck was sitting at the curb.

"Kate—the pickup."

"It's Rudy's," Kate said.

"Yeah. Let's check it out."

They hustled out the back door. No one was around. They were crossing the lawn toward the truck when Michael stopped. "The gear!" He turned back toward the house. Up in his bedroom window, the curtains parted for just a moment. A shadowy figure stood at the window.

They ran into the kitchen, down the hallway and up the stairs. Michael swung open the door. The room was empty. Michael opened the closet. Empty.

"Michael, the gear's gone."

Down on the street, an ignition cranked and an engine rumbled.

They dashed to the window in time to see the pickup driving away. As the old truck rattled down the street, the driver stuck his arm out the window and waved.

"Michael, look." Kate picked up an envelope bearing the CyberTimeSurfer logo. She slipped out the single sheet of paper and read it.

"You have done well in service to the present. The CTS gear will now serve someone else. Good job. Mack."

At the bottom, a hand-written note had been added, "Dear M and K, Remember, life is an adventure. Make of it what you will. Good luck, R."

APPENDIX

Is any of this story true? Yes, much of it is, but not all. Michael and Kate are fictitious. So are Captain Newsome, Private Collins, Joseph Taylor and Meadow. But most important, Lafayette and John Banks were real.

John Banks

John Banks was born in 1750. He and his brother, Jacob, lived on a family farm in Goochland County,

Virginia. Research into Banks family history reveals nothing about John's parents. The story of his father working with horses to buy his freedom is fiction. But it is true that John was not a slave.

John married a young woman named Sally in the spring of 1772 in the "old Episcopal Church." Their first child, James, was five or six when John enlisted in the Continental Army under Colonel Theodorik Bland, who was famous for the cavalry regiment known as Bland's Horse.

No record suggests that John was actually with Lafayette at Barren Hill. The story of his exploits is fiction. But Lafayette did request Bland's help in finding a good horse. Just maybe, John delivered it.

After the war, John and Sally had four more children, Sally, Jane, Judith and John Jr.

In 1818, Congress provided pension money for veterans of the Revolutionary War and John was awarded $97 per year, a considerable sum for the time.

John and Sally grew old together on the family farm. John died at the ripe old age of 94.

In 1845, at age 89, Sally applied for benefits available to widows of Revolutionary War veterans. The application, in the words of the justice of the peace, described Sally as "a respectable old Lady."

In 1850, Sally, at 95 years old, and their son James at 78, still had the farm. Nathaniel Banks, probably a grandson, had an adjoining farm.

In 1855, when Sally was 100 years old, she was granted 160 acres of land in recognition of John's service to his country in the Revolutionary War.

Sally passed away sometime before she turned 105.

The Banks family continued to contribute and achieve. James Banks, born in 1826 and possibly a grandson or great-grandson of John and Sally, became a Virginia lawyer before the Civil War.

The Marquis de Lafayette

Gilbert du Motier de Lafayette (his full name is very long) was born in 1757 into an aristocratic French family. At age two he inherited the title of Marquis, which is akin to being a count or a duke, when his father was killed in a war with the British. When he was 13, his mother and grandfather died, and he inherited one of the largest fortunes in France. But without mother or father, he felt very much alone among his relatives in Paris.

When he was 16, his family arranged his marriage to Adrienne who was only 14 years old. The choice turned out to be perfect and they fell in love.

That same year, Lafayette became the youngest captain in the French army, not because he was a good soldier, but because of his family's wealth and power.

His family's influence placed him in other situations where he didn't "fit in." The new queen, Marie-Antoinette, led an exclusive group of young style-setters. This popular group had a certain way of dressing, acting and talking and they felt superior to everyone else. They always considered Lafayette awkward and often made fun of him. The sting of rejection was worst when he danced with Marie-Antoinette at the Queen's Ball. With all eyes on him, he stumbled and tripped through the dance. Everyone laughed at him and he was deeply embarrassed. No matter how hard he tried, he was not accepted by this "in-crowd." He finally quit trying and decided to follow his own lead.

In 1777, when he was only 19, Lafayette bought a ship and sailed to join America's fight for independence. On that trip he first met Jean-Joseph Gimat.

Again Lafayette's wealth and influence helped his military career and he was made a general in the Continental Army. When he was wounded at the Battle of Brandywine, Gimat was there to carry him off the battlefield.

Lafayette's bravery and leadership impressed General George Washington and other veterans. At just 20 years old, Lafayette was granted his first solo command in May 1778, the excursion to Barren Hill.

The story of Barren Hill is true. The British plotted to trap Lafayette. They marched through the night to surround him, but they woke a militiaman as they passed his White Marsh farmhouse. He rode to warn Lafayette, just as Michael and Kate did in the story.

Lafayette led the escape on the Spring Mill path while one hundred of his soldiers marched in the woods to fool the British into thinking his entire army was preparing an attack. The ruse worked perfectly. Lafayette's army crossed the river at Matson's Ford with only six or seven casualties. He was called a brilliant tactician.

Lafayette served with distinction throughout the war, including at the Battle of Yorktown where the British finally surrendered.

His contribution to America's freedom cost him dearly. He not only risked his life and fortune, but suffered by being so far from home when his little daughter, Henriette, died.

Lafayette's adventures in America made him a celebrity in France. The popular group no longer laughed at him. Instead, they wanted his attention. But by then, he no longer cared. He had followed his heart to more important things.

After America won its independence, Lafayette returned home where the French Revolution was brewing. To avoid bloodshed, he tried to compromise between those who supported the king and those who opposed him. It was a "no-win" situation. Viewed as an enemy by both sides, he was captured and thrown into an Austrian dungeon for five years. He lost everything. He certainly would have died there of sickness and hunger if not for his wife, Adrienne. She persuaded his jailors to let her move into the dungeon just in time to save him.

Lafayette had long believed that slavery must end. He had planned to buy a plantation, teach trades to the slaves and then set them free. He hoped to create a trend that would result in freedom and economic independence for many African American slaves.

But he had lost everything during the French Revolution and was never able to buy a plantation and try out his plan. He continued to believe that slavery must end.

In 1825, when he was 67, Lafayette returned to America, which by then had 24 states. He was the "Nation's Guest" at the White House and was honored by Congress, which voted to repay him $200,000 for his assistance in the cause of American independence. Countless cities and towns saluted him with grand celebrations.

During his triumphant return, he tried to nudge America toward ending slavery by reminding people of the contributions of African Americans. This sentiment he expressed often, as in a New Orleans speech: "I have often, during the War of Independence, seen African blood shed with honor in our ranks for the cause of the United States."

Lafayette also was a hero to the French people, who asked him several times to lead France. But he did not want to rule. He wanted only to fight for liberty for everyone and that he did throughout his life. He died in 1834 at the age of 76.

Should you wish to know more about Lafayette, find the excellent biography by Jean Fritz, *Why Not, Lafayette?* (G.P. Putnam's Sons 1999).

A Few Words About A Few Words

The reader may have questions about a few words spoken by characters in 1778, and a few that remained unspoken. For example, Kate and Michael overheard a British soldier say "hey, presto" to describe how they would capture Lafayette. That phrase was in use by 1735 to indicate a good result obtained as though by magic.

Another soldier used the term "frog." That was, and still is, a derogatory name for a French person. It's used here to add an authentic flavor of how soldiers at war might think of their enemies. Still, despite the value of authenticity, more inflammatory racial epithets have been avoided.

The militiaman, Henry, was fond of name-calling. He called poor George a "goody two-shoes", which meant and still means, one who plays up acting good, without necessarily being so. Henry also called George "chucklehead", "saphead", and "rattlebrain". The meanings are clear. "Cowheart" meant coward. George suggested though, that their troubles were Henry's fault. "That's rich," Henry said, carrying the sarcastic meaning of "you're kidding."

Upon Michael's and John's capture, one British soldier used "ain't." The venerable "ain't" has been in our slang for over two hundred years.

So has "bro." Samuel used it as short for "brother." Here's another modern usage that dates way back. "Bro" was used for "brother" as far back as the seventeenth century.

Finally, Lafayette referred to the "Macaroni Club" when discussing fashion. The Macaroni Club was not really a club at all. Certain young Englishmen of that time dressed in outrageous styles and colors. They had apparently fooled their parents into allowing such dress by saying club membership required it. That's what the old song refers to when Yankee Doodle "stuck a feather in his cap and called it macaroni."

While a time traveler to 1778 would be puzzled by many words and usages, he or she would find a remarkable number of familiar words.